THE PRICE OF SIMPLICITY

Shelagh Taylor

Copyright © 2003 Shelagh Taylor

All rights reserved

The characters and events portrayed in this book are fictitious. Any
similarity to real persons, living or dead, is coincidental and not intended
by the author.

No part of this book may be reproduced, or stored in a retrieval system,
or transmitted in any form or by any means, electronic, mechanical,
photocopying, recording, or otherwise, without express written
permission of the publisher.

ISBN-13: 9798399149394
ISBN-10: 1477123456

Cover design by: Art Painter
Library of Congress Control Number: 2018675309
Printed in the United States of America

In dedication to my mother, whose heartfelt anecdotes help my stories bloom and infuse with a sprinkle of truth.

"You may not control all the events that happen to you, but you can decide not to be reduced by them."
– Maya Angelou

CONTENTS

Title Page

Copyright

Dedication

Epigraph

Introduction

Preface

Lizzie's party	1
Uncovering the sins within	7
Making decisions	15
A new romance	21
Like mother like daughter	30
Love letter	37
Getting caught	41
Tears on her pillow	49
Jack's drug fuelled dreams	53
Learning the system	60
Visiting Order	68
Life inside her prison	71
Owen's Revelation	77
What have you done Patrick?	87
Time for reflection	95

New evidence	99
Home at last	103
Caught in the act	106
Goodbye Father Pie	112
The Phoenix club	117
Patrick finds an ally	121
A visit from Vera	127
Sisters of Mercy	130
Everything comes at a cost	133
Everyone has a weakness	137
The Single Life	145
Things are changing	151
Facing the music	158
Maggie	165
Things go from bad to worse	171
Wedding bells	174
All hail Dougie	181
The pleasure and the pain	185
Sister's united	190
The Acquittal	200
Somebody is watching	204
The price of simplicity	208
Reality comes knocking	217
About The Author	221
The Simplicity Chronicles	223

INTRODUCTION

In the gripping third instalment of "The Simplicity Chronicles" series, the tormented lives of the Ryan family continue to unravel amidst a treacherous web of thrilling suspense and heart-wrenching romance. As the story unfolds, the spotlight shines on Patrick Herron, a priest whose life takes an unexpected turn as he begins a life sentence in the high-security Wakefield Prison.

Within the prison walls, Patrick is ensnared in a world controlled by the menacing UK gang led by the Delaney brothers, Kieran and Chester. Their power extends through coercive measures, forcing inmates to commit unspeakable acts of violence against their fellow prisoners and staff. It is in this hazardous environment that Patrick must navigate his way, treading carefully to protect himself from the lurking predator gangs that always seek to exploit weakness.

Meanwhile, the woman who has held Patrick's heart captive for years, Elizabeth Ryan, grapples with the aftermath of his devastating sentence. Elizabeth slowly finds the strength to rebuild her life and open herself to love again. But as her children grow and the challenges of single parenthood mount, Elizabeth's resilience is tested to its limits. Her newfound love strains her relationship with her mother, creating a painful wedge between them. Yet, as life's trials intensify, unexpected circumstances force Elizabeth and her mother to reconcile and confront their shared past.

Just as Elizabeth seems poised to embark on a future filled with love and happiness, her haunting past resurfaces, threatening to shatter her carefully laid plans. The echoes of her history reverberate, presenting her with a choice that could save her from a predetermined destiny and fracture the life she has painstakingly built.

In "The Simplicity Chronicles: The Price of Simplicity," the Ryan family's saga reaches new heights of tension and intrigue. With gripping thrills and heart-pounding romance, this thrilling instalment explores the depths of human endurance, the power of redemption, and the indomitable strength of love in the face of adversity. Prepare to be captivated as the intricate threads of fate intertwine, weaving a tale that will leave readers breathless until the final page.

PREFACE

'The Price of Simplicity' is the third and most thrilling book in the series, "The Simplicity Chronicles. " It looks at how simply your life can become out of control and the measures you may be forced to take to stay safe both mentally and physically.

The story unfolds with each character dealing in different ways with the acute stress response that prepares us to 'Fight, Flight, or Freeze when faced with the continual battle to deal with the uncertainty of time and the complex nature of things.

I often reflect on my reactions to events and, in hindsight, how I would have dealt with problems differently, if I had been better prepared. Yet, where events collide, glide and shatter your resillience or ability to deal with life differently you make mistakes.

When a significant life change happens, our brains automatically see it as unfavourable, which can affect how we deal with adjustments. Still, mistakes are part of life and we gain experience each time we are challenged to overcome them. We cannot control all events in our lives, but we can decide not to be crippled by them.

I allow most of my characters a chance to reflect and understand the situation they are dealing with more profoundly, simply by looking back on their own existance. I join them on this journey of enlightenment and hope to be a better person because of it.

LIZZIE'S PARTY

As Maggie pressed her nose against the window pane, the steam from her breath formed clouds that condensed onto the glass. She was watching for the first guests to arrive at her sister Lizzie's birthday party. Since leaving Lindley Infants School, Lizzie attended Oakes Junior School, less than five minutes' walk from home. Elizabeth could even see her sometimes at lunchtime from her mending table window, in the schoolyard usually stood on her head. She could always recognise her from the brightly coloured jacket Lizzie loved to wear.

Lizzie's independence had grown so much over the last two years, and she had become a happy child and the class clown. She was popular with her peers and, like her father, could make others laugh. She was a very different girl from the timid, withdrawn child with anxiety issues she had once been.

Now she was having her first party, she had begged Elizabeth to let her have a party reminding her mother that people would stop inviting her to their parties if she never had one back. Lizzie could not wait to get all the gifts that she was expecting. More than anything, she longed for a yo-yo and a set of Jacks or knuckle bones, as some people called them. Elizabeth had prepared some party food adding extra water to the jelly to eke out the measures. As she stirred, she realised it was not going to set. And now the scarlet liquid sloshed about in the dish. The fairy cakes she had made were also a disaster as the tops had burnt, and she had needed to cut them off and get rid of them rather than use the tops as wings. Lizzie didn't mind; the party food looked beautiful, with the brightly coloured paper plates and cups waiting for the eager hands that would soon be grabbing them. Maggie was even more excited than Lizzie; she didn't know Lizzie's new friends and had been planning party games for them all to play. She had drawn a 'Pin-the-tail-on-the-donkey' and stuck it onto the wall in the garden.

Then she had dug some holes in the lawn so they could play crazy golf, with a stick that was shaped like a capital 'L' and a golf ball that she had forgotten to return to the kiosk when she had played crazy golf with her dad in Greenhead Park the previous Sunday. She had taken the three chairs they had outside to play improvised musical chairs and made a mental list of other party games to play once the guests arrived.

Lizzie was dressed in last year's white Whitsuntide dress and a floral headband; she looked like a perfect image of femininity. Maggie had been forced to wear a pretty dress but was already covered in mud from digging the golf holes, and the manic, mud-smeared smile made her look crazed.

Elizabeth was concerned that Maggie was getting too hyped up and hoped it didn't lead to trouble. "Somebody is here!" shouted Maggie with glee as a little girl was ushered along the path.

Lizzie went and opened the door and took the gift from the child, thanking her as she ripped the paper off the parcel, a vast, greedy smile spreading across her face. Lizzie had hardly finished when there was a knock on the door, and another child held a gift for her to devour. Lizzie was expecting five guests, but the mother of the child who had just arrived broke the news that one of the children coming to the party was sick with Chicken Pox. Within fifteen minutes, the other two arrived, and Maggie led them outside to play the first game of crazy golf. The children all loved the game that Maggie had invented, and Lizzie was declared the winner as she had managed to kick the ball in the hole and claimed it fell in.

THE PRICE OF SIMPLICITY

They then played musical chairs, but that was a catastrophe with only three chairs and five children, and one of the chairs broke as soon as three children tried to jump on it at once.

Elizabeth called them inside to eat their sandwiches, drink the jelly from a paper cup and sing happy birthday to Lizzie so she could make a wish blowing out the candles. She gave them each a fairy cake before they were all taken back outside to continue with the party games.

The next game was Pin-the tail-on-the-donkey, and Maggie took charge of fastening a blindfold around each girl's eyes and marking on the paper where they had pinned. Maggie scrutinised the document to find a winner. Seeing hers was far from the mark, Lizzie began disputing where her marker had been placed. The apparent winner started to argue with Lizzie. Still, Lizzie stood her ground with her hands on her hips, declaring that it was her party and she was the winner. Lizzie noticed that as the girl argued, she had to cross her legs simultaneously. This gave Lizzie an idea, and she sprinted as fast as she could to the toilet at the end of the garden, running inside, slamming the door and sliding the bolt across. The girl ran after her, now desperate for the bathroom and started banging on the door and shouting for Lizzie to open up. "I need to wee; open the door." Cried the little girl. Lizzie replied in a stern but sulky voice, "NO!"

The girl started crying as the effects of the lemonade and liquid jelly took their toll on her bladder. Then another girl started shouting that she needed the toilet and began crying. Someone ran inside to get Elizabeth to try and sort it out. In despair, Elizabeth ran down the garden shouting to Lizzie, "Open this door now, Lizzie, or I am sending everybody home."

"NO!" came the unexpected reply. "It is my party, and I want to win every game."

"Lizzie, don't be so mean; these children have bought you lovely presents for your birthday, you have to let other people win, or it isn't fair."

The two girls continued to wail as Lizzie reluctantly slid the bolt to open the toilet. The others all needed the bathroom and tried to get two at a time to relieve themselves. Elizabeth refused to let anyone shut the door in case of another incident.

After everyone had finished using the facilities, Elizabeth led them back towards the house. However, her excitement soon turned to horror when she realised the door must have slammed shut behind her, locking them out. Undeterred, Elizabeth tried the handle, peered through the window, and rattled the door, desperate to get back inside. With tears threatening to spill down her cheeks, she turned to the group of children and explained that they were locked out with no key. Elizabeth slumped onto the doorstep, staring into the distance with defeat trying but failing to think what she could do next.

Maggie stood chewing her gums, thinking of how to overcome this problem mulling idea after idea over in her mind until she suddenly shouted with arms and hands flung upwards, "I know how to get in."

Elizabeth looked at Maggie with suspicion wondering if this was one of her hair-brained schemes that worked in Maggie's mind but nowhere else. Maggie ran over to her mother, dragging her up to a standing position and then pulling her along to the passage between their house and the house behind. "What are you doing, Maggie? Leave Mrs Worsley's door alone?"
"I am leaving it alone. But look, if we lift up the coal hole cover in the passage, and you can lower me down on a rope, I can get upstairs into our house and open the door."

Maggie was jumping up and down in her excitement. She had been thinking about finding a way to get in and out of the cellar without her mother knowing for a while now. She felt that if she could find a rope ladder and climb down, she could sneak up the cellar steps and into the house and frighten her mum. Maggie thought that her mum would think it was hilarious to see her suddenly appear.

Elizabeth needed to be convinced of Maggie's plans. Still, the suggestion of getting her into the cellar seemed possible if only she could find some way of lowering Maggie down the drop.

Elizabeth bent down and pulled up the heavy, round manhole cover. It was hard work, but she managed it. Elizabeth stared into the pitch-black cellar below, noticing that she was too big to fit down, but Maggie wasn't. This idea might work.

Elizabeth took off her cardigan and tied it around Maggie's waist, and she tried to lift her up with it. She couldn't even get Maggie's feet off the ground, so she deliberated that she could not lower Maggie down the hole without fear of dropping her. Elizabeth looked around and saw the washing line. If she could tie one end of the washing line around Maggie and the other end to the house's door handle at the back, that might hold her. Elizabeth asked Maggie if she was sure she wanted to try it, which in hindsight, was a silly question.

Maggie couldn't wait, and when she was tied, Maggie laid on her stomach and scrambled over to the edge of the hole. She dangled her legs down into the cellar below whilst still holding on to the side of the metal rim at the top, and as she could not see what was below her, she just dropped. The strain on the door handle broke it off in the same instant. It hurtled after Maggie; luckily, it missed Elizabeth and got caught on the hole's edge before firing into the abyss. Elizabeth held her breath as she heard Maggie cry and shout, "I made it, Mum. "

Moments later, Maggie limped out of the house, blackened with coal dust, to the party's applause. Her ankle was badly sprained, but thankfully the handle had missed hitting her and hit the cellar wall instead.

The children were so grateful to use the toilet and get inside the house. The immediate drama soon passed, and they all enjoyed a game of sleeping lions, Elizabeth's favourite. At the same time, she cleaned up the party food.

When the children had been collected, Elizabeth explained the circumstances to the parents, using a little poetic licence with the facts. She turned and hugged her children, grateful to Maggie for her help and pleased that Lizzie had enjoyed her party even with the hiccups. The three relived the day's events, laughing at the chaotic twists and turns that seemed to proceed with any family events the Ryan family organised.

Happy and content, the girls went to bed, leaving Elizabeth exhausted and determined that this would be the last party she would host.

As Elizabeth dozed on the settee watching the Liver Birds, she again reflected on how old she appeared compared to the actresses on screen. She needed a man in her life to feel desired and desirable. Things were going to have to change. She daydreamed they would all move away once Patrick was released and finally begin a new life.

Elizabeth closed her eyes and imagined his ravenous touch and her hungry acceptance of his advances. She was so confident of his release that she stayed up late into the night planning where they would go and how it would feel to be with the man she loved every day, especially every night. The fantasies made her gasp with pleasure as Elizabeth imagined his body and hers entwined, finally making love and feeling fulfilled. But the illusion was spoilt as Maggie shouted down the stairs that she needed a drink of water. Elizabeth tutted at the bad timing that Maggie always seemed to succeed in.

UNCOVERING THE SINS WITHIN

Patrick Herron's trial did not go as he had hoped. He had believed it was a clear-cut case, with him as the hero and the others as the villains.

But the case against Patrick for the murder of Jack and the alleged kidnapping of Rosie was not as cut and dried as Patrick had imagined. His solicitor had advised a barrister to defend him as the amounting evidence against Patrick would almost certainly end badly. As the weeks turned into months, he was finally told the trial would be heard at the Crown Court in Halifax. He was left feeling disappointed and defeated.

Patrick had been held on remand and felt oppressed initially by the lack of space and the overwhelming loss of control. He had lived for years in the Spanish mountains, free to roam the vast openness at will, and now here he was in a cell too small to take more than two strides at a time before having to turn. The confinement was driving him crazy. The dull routines, the smell, the excessive noise and the constant fear cannot be imagined unless you have been subjected to the hopelessness of this sort of situation.

In his youth, Patrick had lived in a seminary amongst other males. However, although living in a dorm gives you no privacy, you can roam the grounds and speak out in the open with others. He also knew that living close to other males evoked animal instincts in some men that would have to be handled with care or, failing that, violence. That was the last thing he needed.

Being confined to a prison cell on remand was a distressing experience for Patrick. He was constantly experiencing flashbacks to that night and the days leading up to the murder, keeping him awake at night as he battled with the guilt and the regret of how he had handled the situation. The uncertainty of the trial's outcome and the possibility of losing his freedom caused intense panic, distress, and emotional strain. Being confined in a cell for long periods had become mentally and emotionally draining, creating mind games that drove Patrick almost to insanity. The lack of control and freedom caused a sense of powerlessness and isolation, further exacerbating the emotional toll.

Added to this was how Elizabeth handled everything; he knew her mother would be staunch about losing her only surviving brother. Even the father she loathed would not pass without some regret.

What sort of control would Margaret now exert on Elizabeth to be free of contact with him, and how would Elizabeth react. Patrick knew Elizabeth had faced so much sorrow and hardship in her life, which in some ways had made her more robust but also more vulnerable to the pain of life. Patrick didn't want to cause Elizabeth any more anguish than she had already been through, and yet, he had, even when she had begged him not to.

As Patrick awaited his trial, he had received no word from Elizabeth. He guessed she was awaiting the outcome of the events before daring to make contact. He only hoped it was a positive outcome that at least would stand in his favour.

The night before the murder trial was an incredibly intense and emotional experience for Patrick. He swept through various emotions, including fear, anxiety, sadness, and despair. He felt overwhelmed by the weight of the charges against him, the potential consequences, and the uncertainty of the outcome. Realising that his fate was in the hands of a judge and jury was daunting.

He struggled even more than usual to get any sleep as he replayed the events leading up to the crime in his mind, wondering if he could have done things differently. Again he felt guilty for taking a man's life and remorseful for his actions and the impact they must have had on Jack's family, knowing he had a wife, son, and possibly a daughter.

Then the guilt turned to anger and frustration at being falsely accused of kidnapping and pimping a child when all he had intended to do was save the girl and any others that may have been there or next in line.

When morning finally arrived, Patrick was still awake from hours of torment, prayers and uncertainty. He stepped off the cot and stretched his aching limbs. He shook his head as if to clear away the disturbing thoughts that crowded his mind and waited for the guard to come and unlock the door so he could go and wash away the plaguing images that danced in his mind.

Patrick chose to wear a suit for the hearing and left his dog collar in his cell. While awaiting this trial date, several inmates had asked him to hear their confessions or spoken to him as a priest, knowing the confidentiality that Patrick must retain. This had given Patrick a certain respect amongst the men, and he was at least grateful for this small mercy. Patrick was not one to look for trouble, and these sessions with the prisoners one-to-one were quiet times that had the advantage of stopping his own tormenting thoughts from invading his mind. He listened to the men with sincerity and absolution, advised when he could, and helped pass the enormity of time.

The appearance and ambience of the courtroom were restrained and dignified and added to the tension Patrick felt as he was led from the lower chambers where prisoners are held until requested in court. Then up the well-worn, cold stone step and into the courtroom. All eyes were on a smartly dressed but more haggard-looking priest than he had ever appeared. Sombrely and silently, he made his way to the dock.

Once seated, Patrick scanned the room for Elizabeth, hoping at least she would be there to support him and listen to the evidence that Patrick was sure would be outweighed by the good he had done by taking a considerable risk to rescue Rosie and save her from a life or death by of some unknown abuser. But, Patrick could not see the woman he loved, and his eyes glazed over as he lowered his eyelids and his face towards the floor, lifting his hand up to hold his forehead to ease the pain.

The ones there that had known the priest over the years were shocked by his appearance and looked at him even harder, trying to distinguish if this was due to guilt, remorse or the suffering of an innocent man.

Patrick did not have one person who would come forward to give evidence on his behalf, as the kidnapping and rescue of Rosie were kept secret to avoid the chance of Patrick's plans falling into the wrong hands. The courts tried to add a sexual offences charge to the crime list, but the charges were thrown out as the girl was practically sixteen. Rosie had testified Patrick had dragged her out of the room, and although she had been afraid for her life, she didn't believe he was present at her kidnapping. In addition, Rosie testified that Patrick had never taken any part in her molestation in captivity or beforehand. Rosie wasn't sure if Patrick had any role in planning her capture or imprisonment; she only knew he was the only person there when Jack was killed.

Patrick admitted to shooting Jack intentionally to kill him. Still, he denied any part in Rosie's kidnapping, claiming he was on a clandestine mission to free her. Due to the lack of evidence against Patrick, he was eventually charged only with the cold-blooded murder of Jack Harrison. Patrick received a sentence of life imprisonment that was subject to review later, leaving the court looking like a man convicted of the death penalty. His pallor was ashen, and he hung his head in sadness. Once sentencing began, he never raised his eyes to see those looking down upon him from the courtroom's public gallery.

The realisation hit him as he walked down the court steps to begin his custodial sentence. He had clenched his hands so tightly as the charges against him were read out to the public, with his eyes closed. His throat constricted until he could not breathe; he had not realised that he was drawing blood from the palms of his hands. Bile rose from his stomach and threatened to erupt from his hollow, sunken cheeks to swamp those around him, now staring mesmerised at the man before them.

Most people in the public gallery could hardly contain the excitement of being present at the man's trial that brought down gangland leaders on their doorstep.

The visions of these small-minded people soaked up any scrap of gossip they could glean from what was being said to create fantasies beyond their usual inventiveness to feed to their public in the pubs, streets and homes in the coming weeks.

The onlookers sat with bated breath, their eyes fixed on the events unfurling before them, like the eyes of a rat on its more vulnerable prey. Glistening with glee at the misfortune of others, they may or may not have known but would attest to an almost intimate relationship with whoever would listen to their tall tales. They waited eagerly for any mention of alleged atrocities that they could embellish into crude and cruel details of their own imagination. They resembled vultures perched and waiting for the execution of a man of the cloth, ready to pounce on any gruesome detail that may be revealed.

The movement of bodies leaning forward as Rosie gave her evidence so no juicy snippet was missed was synchronised as if it had been orchestrated. The eyes of the public gallery opened wide on heads that were extended forward to their utmost, mouths almost salivating as their hunger for more intimate details was fed. Smiles flickered around their lips as she spoke of the foreign gentleman that seemed to have disappeared and what he had done to her in the room where she had been held captive. Tears rolled down her childish cheeks that had once been as rosy as her namesake, her innocence lost along with the mother who had adored and protected her since birth.

Rosie told of the fear she had felt when he had entered the room so fiercely and the pain she had felt as he thrust and clawed his way into her underwear with searching fingers. Trying to penetrate her body as he held her so roughly against the wall of her cell.

Rosie had screamed louder than she thought possible, shouting for her mother, fighting for her life, kicking, hitting and biting in her panic for survival. She felt relief when the door banged open, and Jack came to her rescue, dragging the man out and threatening him. Rosie had been so grateful to Jack in that instant. She did wonder later why he hadn't released her when he had saved her from her attacker but imagined Jack had been unable to at that time, and maybe he would come back for her.

As the door had once again been closed and she had heard the lock clicking into the locked position, she could hear shouts from the other side of the door. At first, Rosie thought that she had recognised one of the voices. It sounded so familiar, and in some bizarre way, the voice felt safe because of her recognition.

But the silence again engulfed the almost empty room that had been her prison for the last few days. A dread crept inside Rosie, like dragging ice, freezing its way along her limbs, making her shiver involuntarily and almost uncontrollably. Rosie hugged her arms around her body and felt afraid and helpless; she also felt dirty and violated by the man's probing fingers and her lack of hygiene these past few days. But these were details she could not share in the courtroom, but they lived inside her as memories that had constantly fogged her mind since she had escaped.

Rosie missed her mum so much and felt lonely, afraid and saddened without her there. A few girls her mum had once worked with came along to support Rosie but were also thirsty to hear first-hand what had happened inside the club. Marilyn was one of the supporters, and whenever Rosie felt like she couldn't continue with her recount to the court, Rosie would look up towards the gallery and see Marilyn, with her full make-up on and hair bouffant into the most enormous bun on the top of her head, and the kindest smile on her bright red lips. This would give Rosie strength knowing her mother would have sat next to her with arms linked together, nudging each other and then "oohing and ahhing" throughout the trial.

The events of the past six months had changed Rosie more than she even realised. She had become moody and withdrawn, displaying anger and scorn even toward those trying to help her. She had been passed from one of her mother's friends to another, but each time caused so much trouble they begged someone else to take her.

She was sixteen and legally could live alone if she had an income to support her. Rosie was determined to not be forced to follow her mother's dangerous career even though the offers had dripped in for a place to live in return for her services. Rosie finally decided to join whichever of the armed forces would take her. This was the answer to Rosie's immediate problems: a place to live, food to eat, money to spend and people to take care of her. She didn't care if it was on land, sea or sky as long as she didn't have to be subjected to the touch of a man ever again.

MAKING DECISIONS

As Elizabeth walked into Margaret's house to collect Maggie and Lizzie, Margaret thrust the newspaper at Elizabeth with scorn. She began a tirade about the shortcomings of Patrick Herron. "I hope he rots in hell for what he's done. A priest... tch, more like a wolf in sheep's clothing. I don't want his name to be ever mentioned in the house again after today. Do you understand, Elizabeth? I know he was good to you and that you trusted him, but can you see now how he used people to get what he wanted. Thank God he never had the chance to be alone with Maggie and Lizzie; who knows what might have happened. Did you know he was taking young girls to sell on to despicable beasts like cattle? Ooh, it makes my stomach churn. I could kill him with my bare hands."

"Mum, it doesn't say he took the girl, only that he killed Jack."

"ONLY say's...."

"Only say's 'Your bloody priest,' killed my brother Jack in cold blood. Is that not enough for you, Elizabeth?" Margaret screeched out the words as she seethed in anger.

Margaret continued. "Of course, he took the girl; it is obvious. There was no one else involved. You can be so stupid sometimes, Elizabeth. You believe anything these men tell you."

Margaret ripped the newspaper out of Elizabeth's hands, screwed it into a tight ball and put it on the fire. Nodding as the flames licked around the ball of paper and finally engulfed it.

Elizabeth had read the lengthy custodial sentence in the Huddersfield Daily Examiner with trembling hands, breaking

Elizabeth's heart.

Over the past few years, she had endured immense sorrow and pain, and she felt like she couldn't take it anymore. She didn't dare stand up for Patrick in front of her mother, and she had no one else to turn to for support regarding his situation. Elizabeth felt like a skittle in a never-ending game. Each time she managed to stand back up, someone else came along and knocked her over, cheering at their success and her failure.

Elizabeth had worked through a long and painful day, listening to the gossip at work about the 'Parasite priest' case, as he had been dubbed in the Examiner. She didn't admit to knowing Patrick personally, as this would have raised more than a few eyebrows, but instead sat silently listening without comment. "You are a bit quiet, Elizabeth; what's the matter?" asked one of the menders.

"I just have a headache coming on," answered Elizabeth quickly before any suspicion was aroused. As she journeyed across the road from work that day, she felt ashamed that she had sat and listened to the vile things the women were saying and never once tried to tell them the truth behind the murder. She didn't want anyone to know that she also knew the victim Jack and her grandad Big John.

Elizabeth berated herself as she walked. What had she become to turn her back on her friend and betray his trust? Elizabeth hoped that no one ever did the same to her. She pensively reflected on what she had been taught and what Elizabeth had tried to instil in her children. And, yet, here she was playing Judas. The day couldn't end quick enough.

To be met by her mother's wrath on top of everything else was just too much. Today, when she should have been there to support the man she loved, she acted like a coward and even made excuses to stay away.

She squeezed her mother's arm forlornly, knowing how much she was hurting. Elizabeth shook her head and gave a weak smile, recognising the sorrow of losing a family member. She told her mother she would take the girls home and leave her in peace and quiet. "Why don't you go and see Vera, Mum, she will feel just as sad as you, and it might give you some comfort to talk about Jack?"

"Vera is in Scarborough again; she is never away from the place now. She always was man mad. Vera even talks about getting a flat near the Wallis's Campsite and moving there permanently. But mark my words; she will be back with her tail between her legs when it all goes pear-shaped, and then I suppose I will have to pick up the pieces." Margaret nodded as if she agreed with her statement.

Elizabeth shrugged and walked from the house towards home with the girls arguing behind her every step. They followed her instinctively into the shop on the way home. Elizabeth bought a packet of No6 cigarettes and a large potato to cook for tea. The shop was owned by Maggie's friend David's parents. David's dad Kenneth winked at Maggie, and she attempted to wink back at him, but it was more of a blink. He laughed as he handed over the cigarettes and gave Elizabeth her change. As the three walked down the cobbled street, Elizabeth told them she would make them some 'chats' for tea if they played upstairs until the tea was ready. Maggie and Lizzie cheered. They loved fried potato pieces and would eat them out of newspaper-like chips, which saved on washing up too.

It was cold inside the house, and as Elizabeth shooed the girls upstairs, she dropped her work bag onto the table, taking out the potato that would have to do both girls. She had lost her appetite as emotions went around her head like a washing machine, churning with sadness, distress, concern, and anger.

She began to coil the old newspaper to start a fire, adding a couple of firelighters to the grate beneath the coils. She held the lighted match against the newsprint. She began sprinkling coal bits onto the smouldering paper until the fire took over. Elizabeth sparingly added more coal to warm the house and melt her mood. It felt like winter even though it was only October, and she dreaded the long cold nights ahead, sitting on her own night after night. The thought depressed her, and she suddenly felt furious at Patrick for ruining everything.

When she saw him on her doorstep, and they kissed passionately, she imagined the next step would be making love on the couch or floor. She smiled at this thought, but the pleasant feeling didn't last. He had stopped her, held her back as if she was some sort of hussy, trying to seduce him against his will. Heat flooded her face, and she felt the burning of a blush as she recalled fighting him to kiss him again as he pushed her away. Elizabeth had begged him not to go to the club; why did he always have to be the bloody hero. And now look what has happened. The anger flared up inside her again, and she threw a lump of coal as hard as she could into the fire, sending sparks and burnt ash flying out onto the rug. This made her even angrier as she tried to sweep up the mess and bang the singeing carpet with the dustpan. Elizabeth noticed a little hole in the rug, and that was all it took to set her off crying. Her head bounced as tears leapt from side to side off her nose and chin. She wiped her face with the back of her hand and blew her nose loudly on her handkerchief.

Hearing all the banging, Maggie and Lizzie appeared at the door, asking if the chats were ready. Maggie laughed when Elizabeth

THE PRICE OF SIMPLICITY

turned with her face covered in black ash that must have transferred from her hands when she wiped her face.

Maggie's laughter ended abruptly when Elizabeth marched over to Maggie and smacked her across the face. "Don't you dare laugh at me, Maggie? Do you know how hard I have to work to clothe and feed the pair of you? And, the sacrifices I have made? Get out of my sight, both of you."

Lizzie cried and held onto the back of Maggie's jumper as they walked back upstairs to their bedroom again. Maggie's face was stinging with the slap, but more than the physical pain, she felt hurt by her mother's anger. She had only laughed because her mum's face was smeared in black, and she hadn't meant to hurt her feelings. Her mother had never slapped her face, only her legs and bottom. Somehow this assault seemed far worse, even though it didn't actually hurt any more than being hit on the legs. Maggie sighed and looked at Lizzie, who was still clinging to Maggie and crying. It's ok, Lizzie, it doesn't hurt, honest. I think mummy is sad again. The girls held hands and started singing a song they liked called 'Where do you go to my lovely.' It was a slow and sad song that seemed to fit their mood perfectly.

After a while, Lizzie complained of being hungry. Maggie said she would sneak downstairs and see how their mummy was acting and try to pinch some bread or a biscuit; she told Lizzie to play with her dolls until she got back and not to be scared. Maggie pretended she was a super sleuth, making Lizzie laugh as they saluted each other. Maggie made a big deal of leaving the room with a sweeping motion.

Once the slap had landed on Maggie's face, Elizabeth's anger seemed to subside, and despair set in. She was only thirty-five but felt sixty-five. She had no social life to speak of, two children and predominantly relied on her mother for everything. Danny

19

had moved on; even her aunty Vera had moved on. It was time to decide what she wanted to do with her life next. Patrick would be locked up, maybe forever, for what he had done; she hadn't done anything wrong but fall in love with the wrong man. John Mortimer had been scraping the barrel, but Elizabeth had noticed the overseer at work looking at her and doing his best to flirt with her without the others seeing. It was time to remove some of her walls and let people in so she could start living again.

As the door began creaking open slowly, Maggie's face appeared; Elizabeth could clearly see the imprint of the slap vividly outlined on Maggie's cheek and felt remorse. "I'm just about to start making the chats love; why don't you go back upstairs with a biscuit each for you and Lizzie, and I will shout you down when they are ready?"

Surprised by this sudden turnaround, Maggie went to the cupboard, got two ginger biscuits, and ran back upstairs. Maggie handed one to Lizzie, and they both smiled, relief there had been no more drama.

After the children went to bed that night, Elizabeth decided to write a letter to Patrick explaining how she felt and to let him know after waiting for almost six years for him, she had decided to try and move on with her life. She had no idea where to send the letter. She decided to hand it in at the courthouse when she collected her maintenance money on Tuesday and ask them if they could find out where he was and send it on.

A NEW ROMANCE

When Elizabeth set off for work the next day, she looked different, lighter and younger. She breezed up the road to the mill, clocked in and sprinted up the steps she usually had to drag her feet up. Today Elizabeth intended to flirt back with the hansom, and sexy Robert Duffy, the mending room overseer. Her heart beat quickly at the thought of seeing him, and as she smiled to herself, her lips formed as if she was about to say 'F', with her top teeth gently overlapping her bottom lip. She felt like a burden had been lifted off her shoulders, and she shrugged excitedly at the thought of the day ahead.

Last night as she wrote the letter to Patrick, she swore to herself that these were the last tears she would shed for this man. He was literally out of her reach now, and she may be an old woman the next time he was at liberty to visit with her. She was not an old woman yet, and the fire and passion she had held inside her for Patrick all these years had started to go out. There was a new fire rousing, and she would make sure this was allowed to burn big and bright for all to see. Elizabeth Ryan was alive again; she had risen like a Phoenix from the ashes, as beautiful and captivating as ever.

Elizabeth swept into the mending room, with a smile lighting up her face greeting the menders who worked around her and going into the tiny galley kitchen attached to the mending room to make a coffee to warm her up as she began work.

Robert had spotted her as soon as she walked into the room.

Without realising, he raised his eyebrows in attraction to Elizabeth. He felt the stirrings of desire as he went to the kitchenette to tease her about her evident happiness at spending time at work. Robert, too thought she looked different this morning as if the dark cloud she carried over her head had gone to be replaced with sunlight.

Usually, Elizabeth's eyes would have looked down, and she would have blushed and pushed past him. But today, she raised her eyes to look at him, her smile increasing and throwing him off guard. He made some quip about noticing she was smiling and inquired if it was him she was so happy to see. Elizabeth replied teasingly, "Now, what if it was the reason, Robert?" She made her eyes seem more significant, and her long lashes swept up and down suggestively.

Elizabeth turned on her heel and wiggled her bottom as she walked back to her mending table, laughing, leaving Robert gob-smacked, looking at her in amazement.

"Why are you in such a good mood this morning?" inquired Molly, the mender who had become Elizabeth's friend.

"Wouldn't you like to know, Molly Moran?" grinned Elizabeth as she took out her needles and began work.

Throughout the morning, Robert made every excuse possible to speak to Elizabeth. Each time, she responded like he was the only man in the room. He couldn't understand it, and the lust was driving him crazy. He would have this woman if it was the last thing he did. Molly noticed the number of times Robert came over and commented to Elizabeth, "He fancies you; just be careful."

Elizabeth, still in her euphoric state, replied, "I can handle Robert Duffy; don't you worry. I know how much to give to lead him by the nose and when to stop him so that he is begging for more."

They laughed at this, and Molly quipped, "famous last words", and nodded knowingly.

At Lunchtime, Robert was next to Elizabeth as she went to the canteen to eat her sandwich. More of the menders noticed how close the two were becoming, and Elizabeth felt good that they would be jealous of her. They shared a few laughs and flirted like mad with each other until the whistle went to send them back to work.

Robert plucked up the courage to ask Elizabeth out that weekend, and she said yes. This threw Elizabeth into turmoil; she was brave and forthcoming in the safety of the mending room, but going on a date was different.

Regardless, Elizabeth was excited about dressing up, putting makeup on, and spending time alone without the children. The problem was she would need her mother to babysit, and her mother would want to know every detail about who she was going with and where. Still, needs must, and when Elizabeth went to Margaret's to collect the children after work. As Elizabeth walked into the house, she blurted the request. She did not want to give herself time to make excuses not to go.

Margaret was shocked that Elizabeth would go on a date so soon after all the tragedy regarding her brother. Still, when she heard who it was, she felt relieved. At least the man lived in Huddersfield; Margaret had dreaded Elizabeth meeting someone from miles away like Vera and moving to a distant town with the children. They were all she had left, and she would die if she lost them too. Elizabeth told her mother that she would drop the children at her house on Saturday at seven pm and collect them again on Sunday morning, ready to go to Sunday School. Margaret wasn't very pleased that Elizabeth would be alone all night after spending the evening with a man. She warned her not to be silly this time. "Make sure you don't let him come back to your house for coffee, we all know where that could lead, and the last thing you want is another pregnancy." Then added, "Especially at your age." Margaret looked at Elizabeth to check if the message was sinking in.

All day Saturday, Elizabeth's nerves were on edge, she couldn't decide what to wear, but as they were only going to go for a couple of drinks and not out dancing, she wouldn't need to dress up quite so much. Elizabeth was meeting Robert in the Wellington pub at seven-thirty. She began laying things on the bed as trial outfits. Elizabeth didn't have many clothes; she had never needed them as she had no social life. Maggie and Lizzie appeared at the top of the stairs, which doubled as Elizabeth's bedroom and saw the clothes on the bed. Maggie asked if she would take them to the jumble sale at the chapel, and if so, she could take them for her when she went to Sunday school. Elizabeth stopped, looked up at Maggie, and stared at her. Maggie began to get frightened that she had said something else that would earn her a slap across the face and began backing into her own bedroom.

But Elizabeth wasn't about to hit Maggie; her words made Elizabeth realise that the clothes on the bed were old and only fit for a jumble sale. So instead of being angry and upset, she simply said, "Get your shoes on; we are going to town. It's about time I bought something for myself."

Maggie and Lizzie quickly got their shoes and coats, and Elizabeth got her purse and coat. They almost ran to the bus stop and rode into town on one of the seats at the front of the bus on the upper level. They pretended they were driving the bus and controlling when it stopped and started, and when the girls got bored of this, they began counting all the red cars that passed the bus.

Elizabeth decided she had no time to shop around town and went straight to C&A's. It had been a long time since she did any clothes shopping for herself; most of her clothes were hand-me-downs or so old she needed help remembering, even buying them. As she searched the racks in the shop, Maggie came running over, holding up a white mini-skirt, which was the height of fashion and something Elizabeth would never have chosen. But both Maggie and Lizzie begged her to try it on. It fit perfectly, and she knew she looked stunning with the tight black jumper she had matched it with. To make it even more appealing, it was on sale. Both girls clapped joyfully at how young and beautiful their mother looked. They had never seen her in anything other than dowdy, old granny clothes. She decided to buy the skirt and jumper and smiled all the way home.

She gave the girls beans on toast but only had a slice of toast as she was too nervous to eat. When she got ready and applied her makeup, Maggie and Lizzie danced around the room, cheering. "Don't tell your nanna I have bought this new skirt and jumper. She will go mad if she finds out."

Elizabeth knew the girls loved keeping secrets that only the three shared, so she felt safe knowing they wouldn't say a word. Elizabeth put a long coat over her skirt and top and walked the girls to their nanna's house. She watched them walk through the passage and then made her way to the bus stop further down the road from her mother's, so she wouldn't have a chance to see her in the mini skirt.

When Elizabeth got off the bus, Robert was already waiting for her; he had walked up to the bus stop to meet her, which pleased Elizabeth. She still had the coat fastened tightly around her, and he took her hand as they walked down towards the Wellington pub. Elizabeth took off her long coat when they ordered their drinks and chose a table. Robert's eyes nearly dropped out of his head as he stared at her open-mouthed. He noticed other people looking over and felt amazed that this beauty was with him.

Robert puffed out his chest and raced round to pull the chair out whilst Elizabeth sat down. "You look amazing, Elizabeth."

She smiled and thanked him, feeling self-conscious about revealing so much of her legs. After two brandies, Elizabeth felt woozy and said she would like orange juice. Robert got up to go to the bar, looking back at her as he went.

He had been astonished at how sexy Elizabeth looked when she applied some makeup and dressed up to go out. He was adamant no other men would have her now before him. Knowing her children were spending the night with their nanna, Robert thought he would get her drunk and have more chances to spend the night with her. So instead of orange juice, he bought a double vodka and orange.

After they had finished their drinks, Elizabeth was decidedly drunk; she was slurring her words and could barely walk. He knew she wouldn't make it to the bus stop and went outside to organise a taxi to take them back to Elizabeth's house. He steered her out of the pub, and as she got into the cab, she bent over and was sick all over Robert. As Robert was now covered in Elizabeth's vomit, the taxi driver wouldn't allow him into the cab. Once Elizabeth gave the address, it shot off, leaving Robert at the side of the road covered in spew and smelling disgusting. He had no option but to go home.

Elizabeth stumbled up the path into the house, locked her door and went straight to bed feeling like she was on a merry-go-round, with the room spinning uncontrollably. Never in all her life had she felt like this, and as she passed out, she thought the orange juice must have been off.

She didn't wake up the next day until she heard banging on the door; bleary-eyed, she went downstairs to open it. She was met by her mother looking very indignant like she was about to discover her naked and in bed with a man. Margaret pushed past

THE PRICE OF SIMPLICITY

Elizabeth, expecting to see Robert in all his glory. But when she realised the house was empty apart from Elizabeth, she asked, "Where is he? Did he slink off last night when he had gotten what he wanted? Or this morning when he turned to see the creature from the swamp?"

Elizabeth didn't know what her mother was talking about. She still felt dreadfully ill. Then Margaret continued, "Don't tell me he didn't come back here, your makeup is smeared all over your face, and if that is a SKIRT, then it is almost showing your behind. You were obviously dressing to get raped."

"What's raped?" shouted Maggie over her nanna's voice,
"Get in here and shut the door, Maggie. Do you want everyone to know our business?"

Maggie looked at her mother with makeup smeared all over her face but didn't dare laugh. She looked ill. She felt sorry for her mum; she looked awful and not pretty any more. "My mum's poorly, nanna, can't you see that? She smells just like sick."

Margaret could clearly see that Elizabeth was not very well. Still, she knew exactly the cause and had no sympathy for her. "Go back to bed, Elizabeth. You are a disgrace. The first time you go out alone, look what happens. Do you actually know what happened?"

"No, Mum, I don't. I only had two brandies, and then I asked Robert to get me an orange juice, and suddenly I couldn't walk or talk, and I was sick all over Robert as the taxi drove off and left him standing there."

"Well, thank God you were sick. At least it kept you from losing any more than your dignity. At least you can sleep this off. I will take the girls to Sunday School and leave a note on your door letting Danny know to collect them from my house and drop them off later. Hopefully, by then, you will be dressed in something more than a strip of white material."

Margaret wrote a note for Danny and stuck it onto Elizabeth's door, leaving Elizabeth to suffer in peace. The only saving grace for Elizabeth was that she felt too ill to even think about facing Robert again on Monday. For now, all she wanted was to go to sleep.

Monday morning arrived, and Elizabeth nervously walked up the steps and into work. She sidled into the bench on which she sat to do her mending, her head bent down, turning slightly to say good morning to Molly. Then furtively, looking around for signs of Robert. When she spotted him looking over at her, Elizabeth hid her face out of his line of sight, so he couldn't see the mortified look she had worn since Sunday afternoon when she had eventually been conscious enough to remember the previous night and feel the shame of her actions.

Molly asked her what was wrong and why she was acting so weird, and Elizabeth began to explain. "He spiked your drink Elizabeth; you can't possibly be so ill from two drinks. I bet he had the bartender put some Vodka in your orange juice. At first, Elizabeth didn't believe her. Still, the more she considered the possibility, the more she realised that Molly must have been correct. Elizabeth wasn't in the habit of having a drink, but it made sense that if he had spiked her drink, that would explain everything. She felt disappointed that Robert would do that to her and was simultaneously angry at the upset and shame he had caused.

Robert watched Elizabeth gauging her reactions to the apparent drunkenness on Saturday night. He knew he was in the wrong and shouldn't have tried to get her drunk, but he had been shocked at Elizabeth's strong reaction to the alcohol. He sighed gratefully; at least she had survived the night, but he was disappointed that he had probably blown his chances of bedding this very sexy 'piece of skirt'. As he reflected, he thought, "And what a piece of skirt it was." Robert had to shake his head to rid himself of the image of the white mini skirt and the tight jumper. He could have thrown her over the table there and then in the pub; she aroused him. What a waste...

Elizabeth gave Robert the cold shoulder all day. She had expected him to come over to see how she was, at least, or apologised somehow. But, he had stayed clear apart from the times he had to speak with her regarding work and how he had blushed as she stuck out her chest in defiance.

The next day after fully recovering from her drunken episode, Elizabeth felt herself again. She was determined to make Robert jealous and flirt with anyone and everyone she could. The thought brought a mischievous smirk as she walked up the steps to the mending room.

Despite being busy all morning, Robert was the first to go to the kitchen during the break. He was still guilty about what he had done but determined to make amends, even if it meant getting nowhere. Remembering that Elizabeth liked her coffee milky, he made her a cup and placed it in front of her as she chatted with Molly.

Robert's frustration grew, but he tried to brush it off and focus on his work. Despite his efforts to win Elizabeth, he still had a long way to go. Elizabeth thanked him, but as Robert walked away with a smug grin, he overheard the two women snickering and laughing, leaving him to wonder if they were laughing at his expense.

LIKE MOTHER LIKE DAUGHTER

When Elizabeth hadn't turned up to pick the children up on Sunday morning, Margaret had been sure it was because she was still in bed with the overseer at work Robert Duffy.

Margaret was furious that her daughter was acting like a wanton woman. She told no one in particular, "Elizabeth is sex mad like her aunty Vera. "Margaret had decided to march the children home and confront the two adults. Margaret had thought that they would still be fornicating like animals. Well, she was going to ruin that sort of fun. It was disgusting.

When Margaret had been confronted by Elizabeth, still dressed in the shortest skirt she had ever seen and looking ill, Margaret had been convinced that Robert was still there. But when Elizabeth explained the orange juice, it made more sense.

Once the girls were at Sunday School, Margaret decided to make an egg custard, hoping that Elizabeth was feeling well enough to eat something by tea time. The egg custard should help settle her stomach, which triggered a memory of a similar situation.

When Margaret split up from Charles, Elizabeth's father, it was due to his infidelity with another woman. This had almost broken Margaret, the shame and humiliation of losing her husband to a woman that, in her opinion, was a poor second best. Still, her ego was severely damaged, and when he didn't do everything in his power to get her back, she was shocked into taking measures herself. Margaret needed to know she could get Charles back if she wanted to. She felt compelled to seek proof that she was more desirable than the other woman.

Margaret kept her struggles to herself, fearing the possibility of failing and looking foolish. She constantly felt sad and lacked energy, often needing to sleep more than usual. She had visited the doctor, who suggested she may suffer from depression, a newly recognised disorder. The doctor prescribed some tablets to help her calm down and told her to try and get plenty of free air and exercise. However, despite the suggestion, Margaret refused to accept that it was depression due to the stigma still attached to mental illness.

Margaret began the tablets but also started plotting how she would try to lure Charles away from (The Blonde), Margaret's name for the adulterous woman who had stolen her husband. When he had called to collect Elizabeth at the arranged time, Margaret had slipped a note into his hands. With lips firmly closed and looking at Charles, she shook her head slightly from side-to-side to indicate silence. Margaret guessed he would read the note as soon as he had left the house and raced upstairs to watch him as he walked down the path and away from the place they had shared as man and wife. She saw him unfolding the note and reading before he turned and looked back at the house. Margaret hid behind the curtain, unsure if he had spotted her furtively watching him as he departed with their daughter.

When Charles brought Elizabeth home at around five that afternoon, he handed Margaret a note looking at her deeply, and she thought lovingly. When the door closed behind him, she tore open the message Charles had sealed in an envelope. The letter agreed to meet with Margaret, and he suggested they meet that evening to share a drink and discuss things amicably in private. It said he would meet her on the road outside the house at seven

SHELAGH TAYLOR

that evening and walk up to the 'Field head' pub, where they could have a drink, relax and talk privately.

Margaret was surprised that she felt giddy at the thought of this clandestine meeting and hummed to herself as she ran up the stairs to choose the correct outfit for the occasion. She wanted something that showed off her best features: her ample bosom and curvy hips. Make-up would transfer the mummy's face into a desirable feature. Margaret hummed in excitement; she felt young again and exhilarated as if she was going to meet a new beau.

But he wasn't a new beau; he was a cheating husband, HER, cheating husband. As much as she had been motivated and thrilled to meet up with him secretly, she wanted him to hurt like she had. He was not just a bit put out but really hurt, so he realised what he had forsaken.

Margaret also wanted to make the cheating, thieving woman who had deliberately stolen what was hers suffer. Margaret's glowing face turned to one of scorn when she thought about the pain and humiliation she had felt. Margaret would not allow herself to be a soft and soppy girl. She was a strong woman who didn't need the love of a man in her life. In those moments, she almost convinced herself this was true, as she went downstairs to tell her mother she had an errand to do that evening and would be late back.

As Margaret left the house to meet Charles, she looked enticing. She had swept her voluminous hair around in a chignon and made her lips plump up with the scarlet lipstick. Her dress was a gingham that was fashionable with the fitted bodice and flared skirt, red stiletto heels, red scarf and gloves; Margaret looked every inch a woman to be desired. Her Beaver Lamb fur coat covered the dress to keep out the chill and ensure she looked classy.

THE PRICE OF SIMPLICITY

Charles watched as she walked up the garden path and onto the road, knowing she was far more beautiful and desirable than Freda. Still, her coldness had been too much to tolerate. Freda was always warm and alluring, working hard to please him and ensure he had everything a man could want. Freda was aware of how beautiful Charles's wife was, and she had to make sure he didn't regret leaving his wife and moving in with her. She would do anything to keep him now that she had him in her home. Her son needed a father, and they looked like a respectable family with Charles around.

He kissed her on the cheek when she reached him but felt awkward as they began to walk along the road to the pub. Charles was curious about what she wanted to discuss and assumed it was either the house or Elizabeth. He was nervous that she would demand money from him to keep either of them. This wouldn't go down too well with Freda, who dreamed of moving onwards and upwards with Charles at her side. She was ambitious and knew ways to make it hard to say no.

When they walked into the pub, Charles went to the bar whilst Margaret went to sit in a booth. Charles knew Margaret didn't drink but thought if he could loosen her up a bit, he might be able to persuade her to sell the house and give him half. Charles knew it was her right to stay in the home and make him pay half of the mortgage. But Charles needed to sweeten her up and avoid this happening. So instead of the usual orange juice, he ordered her a gin and orange, a beverage that was hard to detect if you were unaware.

Sitting at the table, they talked about Elizabeth for a while, and the conversation was kept civil. It wasn't long before Margaret began to loosen up with the effects of the gin and was laughing and flirting more than he had ever seen her do before. Margaret became more tactile as she spoke and held his hand, fluttering her eyes at him. She began to make lustful suggestions about maybe rekindling their youth outside. As Margaret leant over his arm, her body became heavy, and her breasts brushed against him.

Charles liked this new Margaret and went to the bar in the pretence to get her another orange juice and bought a double gin to add to the orange juice.

Further persuasion was unnecessary; he led her from the table and outside as soon as she finished her drink. Margaret was having a lot of trouble coordinating her legs, and her words sounded distant and slurry to her ears. She clung to Charles, and they began walking toward home. Charles began to kiss her, and when Margaret demonstrated no resistance, he pulled her into the snicket at the top of Longwood Edge. As the kissing became more passionate, Charles put his hand up Margaret's skirt pulling her underwear down, the excitement was driving him crazy, and he thrust himself into Margaret as she slumped on his shoulder. She was too drunk to stop him or even care as she felt the vomit rising from her stomach, making her thrust back and forth. Charles took this as a sign of pleasure, making Charles lose control. He ejaculated into Margaret as her vomit erupted from her mouth over herself and Charles.

When he realised what she had done, he pushed away from Margaret, but she clung to him for dear life, unable to stand up alone. He tried desperately to clean himself and hold her up simultaneously. Eventually, he gave up trying, and they wobbled out of the snicket onto the road. He had to almost carry Margaret back to the house and escort her to the door, where he left her on the step. Charles knocked on the door loudly and left Margaret to make his way back to Freda with a lot of explaining to do.

Margaret dry heaved and began knocking on the door herself. Eventually, her mother opened the door, took one look at her and exclaimed. "Margaret, you are drunk!"

Margaret all but crawled inside the house and up the stairs to bed.

The next day she felt so ill she told her mother they would have to get the doctor. Her mother scoffed and asked her if she had made any more mistakes last night as her stockings were in shreds, and mud was all over her fur coat. When Margaret continued to moan about feeling ill, her mother repeated that this was the effect of too much alcohol, not an illness, but a consequence. Margaret had never been drunk before and knew she had only drunk two orange juices and told her mother so.

Then the memory hit her like a sledgehammer. She recalled being up against the wall and having sex with Charles and then being sick all over him. Margaret knew no protection had been used as she could feel the evidence all over her legs. She prayed to God that she had not been impregnated in this inane attempt at revenge. How could she have been so stupid?

Another thought hit her then. What if Charles had passed on a venereal disease from that hussy he lived with? All she had intended to do was make a pass at Charles, make him realise how sexy she was, lead him on until he left Freda then shun him. So he would lose both women, hurting him like he had hurt her.

Looking back, she could see the similarities of her daughter being drunk after being duped into it by her naivety. She remembered being ill for days after her drunken night out with Charles. Thankfully it did not end in a pregnancy, he and Freda remained together, and she left the house that she had loved so much when she had married Charles.

Thinking about Elizabeth, she realised that she had made the same mistake trying to be a sexual temptress to lure a man but not having the experience or ability to live that kind of life. If she could only turn the clock back, she would have done things differently, been more aware of her husband's needs, tried harder to please him, and put him first like a wife should. But she was not that person and realised too late that looks are only skin deep. The type of women who run off with married men don't have to be more beautiful, but they do have to be more forgiving and self-sacrificing to get and keep what they want. Margaret felt sorry for Elizabeth, knowing what she had tried to do with the short skirt and make-up, but it had backfired. She only hoped that Elizabeth wouldn't live to regret it later.

Margaret was pleased to see that Elizabeth was moving on with her life. She was no longer dwelling on her past or hiding behind a religion that had not served her well. Elizabeth realised that her children needed a reliable father figure in their lives. While Robert Duffy might not be the ideal choice, Elizabeth knew that she had to take action and find someone soon, or she risked being left on the shelf as a bitter old maid.

LOVE LETTER

Elizabeth had taken the letter she had written to Patrick when she went to collect her maintenance and handed it over the counter, asking them if they could find out which prison Patrick Heron was in and kindly send the letter on for her. They had all but laughed in her face. "We are not running a postal system, love. You will have to post it yourself."

Elizabeth blushing and aware that the other people in the queue were desperately trying to hear what she was saying, replied. "I would if I knew where he was, but I don't."

The lady behind the counter said, "That is not my problem, love. You are in the wrong department for finding out addresses of PRISONS." She said the word loudly, causing Elizabeth even more embarrassment.

"We are dealing with incoming and outgoing money, not love letters. She scoffed at her words and shouted, "NEXT," ending the conversation with Elizabeth.

Elizabeth left the building feeling like the scum of the earth. She needed a coffee and a sit-down and went on to the 'Wimpy Coffee Bar'. Elizabeth ordered a coffee and sat down, looking forlornly at the letter still clutched in her hand. Elizabeth needed to figure out what to do with it, where to send it or even if she should.

Elizabeth had decided to start seeing Robert Duffy and move on with her life. Still, she wanted closure on one romance before she could give a new one her full attention. Elizabeth sat sipping her coffee; when she felt a hand on her shoulder. Startled, she looked up. "I've been saying your name Elizabeth. You must have been miles away." Announced Marilyn as she stood towering over the table with a milkshake.

"Oh, Marilyn, yes, I was miles away. I am so happy to see you; you may be able to help me."

Marilyn sat down opposite Elizabeth. Before she could speak, Marilyn gushed, "Have you heard about that priest that you used to fancy, Father Herron? My God, I was in court every day. Poor Rosie, do you remember Ruby? Rosie is her daughter, or should I say she 'WAS' her daughter. She was found dead, not Rosie but Ruby. You wouldn't have believed the dreadful state of affairs unless you'd heard it with your own ears. Anyway, love, how can I help you?"

Elizabeth stared at Marilyn, unsure what to say or how to say it. She admitted hesitantly that she had heard and wanted to get him a letter. "A letter, what sort of a letter? He's in prison, you know that don't you?" replied Marilyn.

"Well, yes, but I don't know which one, and I thought if you were going to visit him, perhaps you could take it and give it to him." Stuttered Elizabeth.

"Visit him. Are you crazy, Elizabeth? After all the publicity, can you imagine that his only visitor is a man in a skirt and a wig with bigger balls than most of his cellmates? I don't think he would thank me, do you?"

Marilyn was always terribly nosy and insisted on knowing why Elizabeth was writing a letter to Patrick. Without barely a breath, Marilyn quizzed Elizabeth and chatted away, congratulating the café owner on the delightful milkshake.

THE PRICE OF SIMPLICITY

"Oh, I … Well I… Elizabeth was at a loss for what to say, so she said, "I wanted to wish him well."

"Marilyn guffawed at this statement. "Wish him well! He's in prison doing life, not embarking on a new career. Well, he will be starting a new career but not one of his choosing. My God, Elizabeth, you always were naïve. Heaven help us."

Elizabeth sat stunned into silence and wished she had never spoken, feeling sick to her stomach after the rebuffs she was getting today. Marilyn piped up again. "Hey, did you hear they pulled down the row of houses on Kilner Bank where we used to live? I had no idea there were so many rats in those houses. Florrie Smith told me it was like a black river running down the road with all the rats escaping from beneath the houses and toilet blocks. When I think about all the times I have been against the toilet block wall with a punter, rats must have been running all around. It makes me shudder."

There was no stopping Marilyn once she started, and she continued with barely a breath in-between. Do you remember Stanley Mullin, the old guy that used to beg outside the mill on payday? Well, Florrie told me that the smell from his house was terrible this summer, and she went round to ask him to get rid of whatever was stinking the street out. She said she looked through the window and could only see a black man sitting in a chair, no sign of Stanley."

Marilyn took a sip of her milkshake and then continued. "Florrie banged on the door, and no one answered, so Florrie left it. A few days later, it was another hot day, and the smell was like rotting meat. She had just put some washing out and didn't want the stench clinging to the clean sheets. She marched back round there. Ironically she thought the smell would attract rats." Marilyn laughed at her own joke before continuing. "Well, the same man was sat in the same chair, and even though she banged and shouted, nobody answered the door. Florrie was livid. Off she went down the street, where there happened to be a beat cop walking up the road. She told him about the smell and the black visitor that hadn't moved and said something was amiss. The police officer returned with her and said he would force the door. When they went inside, the man's face appeared to rise. It was 'Blue Bottles' that had been on his face, and when they lifted up, Stanley's face was alive with maggots and a big black rat was sat on his chest eating his nose."

That was all Elizabeth could stand. She jumped up, ran to the toilets and was sick, heaving and heaving until nothing was left. With her eyes running, she returned to the café and told Marilyn it was nice to see her, but she had to go. Elizabeth picked up the letter and walked outside, dropping the note into the rubbish bin under the careful eye of Marilyn, who watched her, wondering what was in the letter.

GETTING CAUGHT

As she stuffed the letter for Patrick into the bin, Elizabeth decided to stop her past life and move on. Marilyn's story had made her physically sick, and the stories of the rats deserting her old house on Kilner Bank saddened her, leaving a feeling of loss and grief again. It was time to stop living in the past and turn to a better future for her and her children.

Elizabeth had fancied Robert from afar for a while now. He was the first man she had even looked twice at since Patrick, and gradually as the weeks passed, Elizabeth succumbed to Roberts's charms. The two started dating, but Elizabeth was determined to keep his sexual advances at arm's length until they had a more formal relationship. She had been indoctrinated into the Catholic faith. Although she would have gladly thrown all inhibitions and teachings out of the window for a chance to lie naked with Patrick, Robert had shown he was not to be trusted. Therefore rules were needed to keep rash and most likely bad decisions at bay.

As Elizabeth's and Robert's relationship grew, so did the sexual fervour. But Elizabeth was adamant she would need a ring before she ultimately submitted to Robert's charming and hard-to-resist advances. It was beautiful to feel so desired and experience the touch of a man after such a long time. Even so, she was a little afraid. Elizabeth was not so embarrassed about Robert seeing her naked; she knew she still had a shapely body. What she most feared was leaving him disappointed when she finally gave in to his lust. Elizabeth lacked experience in sexual relationships, especially for a woman her age. Elizabeth didn't know many things the women discussed in the mending room. Elizabeth always pretended to be appalled by the talk, as she didn't want the others to realise her naivety. She longed to ask questions and gain insight into how to please a man. Listening to these women talk, they could arouse any man living and used terms for their tricks that Elizabeth found alien. One particular phrase had Elizabeth dumbfounded and exposed her as not knowing its meaning.

The menders had been hunched together at lunchtime, and she heard one say she would like to blow Robert. Elizabeth's ears pricked up at the mention of his name, and she turned to join in the conversation. Knowing that Robert and Elizabeth were an item, the mender who had said it quickly tried to change the subject. Still, Elizabeth piped up, "What do you mean blow Robert?"

Thinking there would be trouble, the other menders all went quiet and looked at the two women. "Blow him where?" Elizabeth's curiosity had been piqued, and she wanted to know what was funny about blowing air onto someone. "What will blowing on him achieve?"

The silence was deafening as the others waited eagerly for the mender to explain what she meant to Elizabeth. "I meant I would blow him down the stairs if he gives me any more bad work." luckily, she realised that Elizabeth had no idea what a 'blow-job' was. So told a lie that, at the moment, sounded convincing to her ears.

Elizabeth shook her head, puzzled but accepted the explanation. The others all looked at each other incredulous that a woman of Elizabeth's age had no idea what the mender had actually meant.

Elizabeth had to admit she was falling for Robert. However, he was still her boss at work, so Elizabeth did not mention the idle threat of the woman complaining about him at break time. Elizabeth didn't want to become a tell-tale and lose the trust of the other menders. She hadn't realised that Beryl, the mender who made a comment, had her eye on Robert and wanted to bag him for herself. Beryl assumed if she made Robert happy sexually, he would ensure she had all the best work and didn't know why Elizabeth wasn't using her advantage to get the better jobs on offer.

Robert had two children that he shared custody of, and it was his weekend. He and Elizabeth arranged for her to take Maggie and Lizzie to his house on Saturday afternoon to introduce the children. This would be the first time the children would meet and the first time they were made aware of their parent's courtship. The understanding was that they would all have tea together, and then Elizabeth would take her girls home. If all went well, Robert and Elizabeth would take all the children to Blackpool for the weekend as the next step in their relationship. Surprisingly the tea went well, the children got along, and everyone seemed ok knowing their parents were dating. Of course, the weekend away in Blackpool sealed the deal.

Robert booked the weekend break at a boarding house with two double rooms and a box room for his son. He told the house's landlord they were a married couple with four children, three girls and one boy. Robert intended to share a room with Elizabeth, the three girls could share a room, and his son Mark would have the box room.

But when they arrived, Elizabeth had other ideas. Much to the landlord's surprise, who had assumed they were a married couple, Elizabeth refused to share a room with Robert. The landlord nodded his understanding, thinking they must have fallen out, and the wife was playing hard to get. Robert was furious about Elizabeth choosing to rebuff him yet again but kept his temper, thinking perhaps Elizabeth would soften.

Elizabeth ended up sharing a room with her girls, Robert had the other room with Mark, and his daughter Sharon had the box room.

He tried everything he could to get Elizabeth to himself and leave the children to their own devices. Maggie and Lizzie had never been given freedom and went wild.

Saturday afternoon, after they had unpacked and were told by Robert that they could all go out alone. They were within walking distance from Blackpool Pleasure Beach, where they ran to get there and spend any money they had.

Once the children left, Robert entered Elizabeth's bedroom and tried to seduce her, kissing and petting her. She laughed but pushed him away, telling him to stop as the children might walk in. He informed her they were alone as he had given each of them a shilling to spend and sent them out to play. Elizabeth went mad, demanding to go and find them before they were kidnapped or murdered. Pushing Robert out of the way, she ran past him and made her way to Pleasure Beach.

Finally, she spotted the children and made them all return to the digs where they were staying. Lizzie had spent the shilling and all the rest of her spending money in the first five minutes and had to be dragged back to their room. Robert and Elizabeth had a blazing row, and both spent the rest of the day with their children up and down Blackpool front.

That evening when they all returned to the rooms, Robert apologised to Elizabeth, and they all went out to tea. She agreed they would send the kids to bed early and spend time together. All the girls went into Elizabeth's room, Mark was sent to the box room to read a comic, and Robert went and bought a bottle of sherry from the off-license.

The two adults had a drink and enjoyed being alone together.

THE PRICE OF SIMPLICITY

Elizabeth felt in control, knowing how much sherry she was drinking. At the end of the evening, Robert coerced Elizabeth into his room, and they lay on the bed, cuddling for a long time. When things got too steamy, Elizabeth stopped it and said she was returning to her room. "You have to be patient, Robert; I'm not that kind of a woman."

Robert was fed up with the constant rebuffs and teasing behaviour. He decided when they returned home, he was going to re-think things. Robert wasn't sure he wanted to stay with a woman who offered no sexual pleasure and thought she might be frigid, and if so, he was making a big mistake.

The next day they all went out together and caught the train home, the spark seemed to have gone for Robert, and he was quiet all the way back. At Huddersfield Railway station, they said their goodbyes and each headed to their own homes. On the way, Robert dropped his children off at their mum's house and headed into town. He needed a drink and a laugh, and knowing the flirty Beryl would be in the Wellington pub, he called in to chat her up and maybe get a feel for free. Robert surmised that Elizabeth need never know and what she didn't know wouldn't hurt her.

On Monday, Elizabeth went to work excited to talk to Molly about her weekend away, she was running a little late, and when she arrived, Elizabeth sensed an atmosphere in the mending room. Molly had put her head down and pretended to be deep in concentration. Elizabeth noticed the others kept looking over at her. Robert was nowhere in sight, and the only person in a good mood was Beryl, who was waltzing up and down the room singing, dancing or humming.

"What's gotten into her this morning," Elizabeth asked Molly. Beryl overheard her and came over.

"It's not what's gotten into me this morning that should concern you, Elizabeth. It's what got into me last night." Beryl howled with laughter at her joke as she sidled off to annoy someone else.

Elizabeth turned and said to her friend, "She must have trapped another poor man last night by the sounds of it. What do you say, Molly?"
Molly just grimaced and continued working.

Just before the break, Robert had brought Elizabeth a new piece to work on and removed the one she had finished. He looked at her sheepishly, and she winked at him, making him blush. Robert looked relieved and gave an audible sigh of relief. Elizabeth was puzzled by his behaviour and looked at him questionably. Elizabeth looked across at Molly and shrugged. Robert said, "Busy morning for me today. Keep up the good work, you two."

He waved from behind as he wheeled the cart with the completed piece away. They both got up to go to the canteen for morning break taking their empty cups and a bag each of instant coffee, powdered milk and sugar mixed with them.

When they had rinsed their cups and made fresh coffee, they sat down, Molly had remained quiet all morning, and Elizabeth was concerned that she had troubles. "What's wrong, Molly? You seem... I don't know; somewhat vacant today. Has something bad happened over the weekend?"

Molly looked at Elizabeth and said quietly, "There's something I need to tell you, Elizabeth, and I am unsure how to do it."

"What on earth is the matter, Molly? Is it something serious?" inquired Elizabeth.

Just then, Beryl walked up to the table and said in a voice loud enough for everyone to hear. "Has he confessed his sins to you yet, Elizabeth? I'm guessing not when you didn't tear his eyes out when he took your piece away."

Molly shouted to Beryl, "Leave it, you vicious, nasty bitch."

Others in the room agreed. "You've had your fun, Beryl. Now just give it a rest. It's hardly cutting news that you've shagged somebody else's boyfriend, AGAIN, is it? It's nothing to be proud of."

Elizabeth looked from one to the other as the penny dropped. Robert must have slept with Beryl last night. Tears raced fast and furious into Elizabeth's eyes as she fought to hold them back as she raced from the room to the toilets. Molly ran after her, trying to comfort her as Elizabeth went. "You know what Beryl is like, love; she probably threw herself at him when he felt vulnerable. Wash your face, and we can sit at our tables with our coffees. I will go and get them now and give that scheming bitch a piece of my mind whilst I am there."

Elizabeth ran into the toilets, slammed the door, and cried. She berated herself as she sobbed. "How could I be so stupid to put my faith in a man who had already proved himself untrustworthy. Oh, Elizabeth, you stupid, stupid, silly woman."

Elizabeth needed to walk back to her board and get back to work. She had to pull herself together. She coaxed herself. "Come on, you can do it, one step before the other."

Elizabeth stood up from over the sink, washed her face once more, brushed her hair back with her hand and marched from the toilets and back to her bench. Molly leaned across and squeezed her arm, "Good girl, love, he wasn't worth it if he let that whore tempt him anyway."

Elizabeth smiled gratefully and began work. Robert watched from behind some boxes regretting his Sunday night fling with Beryl. He knew he had lost Elizabeth, and Beryl was not worth it. She was willing and eager, but she was anybody's for a brandy and who wanted a woman like that in their life. He kicked himself for being impatient and not waiting for Elizabeth because he knew Elizabeth would be more than worth the wait from the kisses and cuddles he had managed with her. Robert dreaded seeing her with another man, and he wasn't silly enough to think she would not be swooped up now she was single again. Rebound love was what Robert called it, and someone was always waiting in the wings to save a distressed maiden. If only that bloody, stupid bitch had kept her mouth shut, he could have made a life with Elizabeth and had as much afternoon delight as he wanted if he had married her. What a bloody waste!

TEARS ON HER PILLOW

Elizabeth got through the day the best she could. The other menders were really good and gave her the support she needed whilst snubbing Beryl, the trouble stirring, floozie. Robert kept a low profile near Elizabeth but took an opportunity later that day to corner Beryl and give her a piece of his mind. "You big-mouthed, fucking whore, why did you have to start bragging about a quick and drunken Sunday night shag. You might be proud of it, but I certainly am not. You were the worst shag I have ever had, and I regretted it the moment it was over. You are a dirty whore and nothing more. Don't you dare say another word about me to anyone, or you will live to regret it. You will be down that yard with your cards as fast as you can say 'Jack Robinson'."

A few of the others heard Robert shouting the odds at Beryl, and some did feel a bit sorry for her. But she had been a fool to herself to tell all and sundry about shagging Elizabeth's boyfriend. Beryl had done it intentionally to show off, and it had backfired big time. Most of the other menders were not speaking to Beryl, Robert had it in for her, and she hadn't got the man she was after, even after dropping her knickers.

Elizabeth had worked the rest of the day in shame at everyone knowing her business and what a fool she had been. Elizabeth could feel them laughing at her and saying how naïve and ridiculous she had been to think she could keep a man like Robert on a string like a yo-yo. In her head, Elizabeth could hear their words. "She never could keep a man. She has no idea about life. Who is going to want her now?"

Molly tried her best all day to make Elizabeth feel better; she was a good friend and felt terrible about what had happened. Her husband had had numerous affairs before he died suddenly of a heart attack. Molly knew how Elizabeth must be feeling. The hurt, rejection, and humiliation all returned to her and stung her again. She guessed Elizabeth would cry herself to sleep tonight, just like she used to do every time she found out he was doing it again. It felt like being soiled or dirtied somehow and unable to wash it away. Like someone taking your underwear and wearing it, then handing it back and blaming you for the stains. It was a dreadful feeling, poor Elizabeth, to go through that on top of everything else that had happened to her.

Thankfully Robert had kept out of the way once he was aware that Elizabeth knew about him and Beryl. He would leave it today and try and apologise tomorrow. Robert knew she wouldn't forgive him, but he wanted her to see that he was sorry, at least. As Robert tried hard to focus on his job, he sighed and said quietly to himself. "What a bloody day."

As Molly said goodbye to Elizabeth at the clocking out machine, Molly squeezed Elizabeth's arm because Molly didn't know what else to do that would help. As Elizabeth ambled over the road to collect her children, a dark cloud hung over her, weighing her down.

She was greeted with a light-hearted welcome when she walked through her mother's house door. "How were the two love birds today, then. Did you talk about your weekend away?" One look at Elizabeth's face alerted her mother that the day had not gone so well after all.

THE PRICE OF SIMPLICITY

"It's over, mum; he's been sleeping with that Beryl from the mending room. I have never been so humiliated. She told everybody all about it this morning. I felt a right fool sitting there whilst she bragged about sleeping with the man I had just been to Blackpool with."

That was it. The floodgates opened, and Elizabeth cried into her pinny covering her face. Maggie and Lizzie looked on, unsure what to say or do. Margaret looked at her daughter and shook her head, saying, "They are all the same, Elizabeth; the quicker you find that out, the quicker you'll learn not to trust them."

"Oh, Mum, I feel such a fool."

"You are a fool Elizabeth, like the rest of us," quipped Margaret.

Elizabeth collected the girls, and they walked home. Maggie and Lizzie knew to keep out of the way and leave their mother to grieve alone. They played upstairs, and Maggie suggested they make their mum a mask to cheer her up. So, they began colouring and cutting out the paper until they had a face mask for their mother. Maggie crept downstairs and pushed it under the door for her mother to find when she had finished crying. Maggie returned upstairs, and Lizzie sat on the bed and talked about Robert. "I didn't like him anyway, did you, Lizzie? He was too bossy. At least he won't be our new dad now." Both girls smiled at this and played a fun game.

Maggie heard her mother crying that night as she lay in bed. She slipped out of the covers, entered her mother's room, and inched her way into the single bed beside her mum. "Don't be sad, Mum: me and Lizzie still love you ." This made Elizabeth cry even more, finally falling asleep.

The next day as Elizabeth opened the door to go to work, the postman was there, and he handed her a letter with an unfamiliar postmark that Elizabeth stared at until recognition dawned on her.

JACK'S DRUG FUELLED DREAMS

It was unlikely he would ever see Elizabeth again, she had not attended court for the hearing or sentencing, and he hadn't received any word from her. Patrick would have to finally accept that he would never have the woman he loved in his arms again, but she would remain in his dreams.

He lay on the cot in his cell and thought about when Jack had begged Patrick to help him overcome his demons. He wasn't a Catholic but explained to Patrick that his recurrent dreams were so frightening that he needed to confess at least a few of his sins to have an opportunity to sleep without torment.

Patrick had hardly been back from Spain a week when, out of desperation, Patrick had gone to see Jack to try and find Elizabeth and had stumbled upon some papers that, at the time, Patrick was unsure of. He met with Jack soon after to hear his confession. After meeting up with Cameron Murphy, the absolute truth behind Jack's activities came to light. Patrick had regretted giving the man any sort of comfort, knowing now the man's true intentions.

Patrick knew that Jack had started to use Heroin to help him cope with his failing business. The night terrors he was experiencing were more than likely due to the effects of Heroin as opposed to his guilty conscience, which Patrick doubted he possessed at all.

Patrick decided to humour the blood-related man to Elizabeth and possibly get a deeper understanding of the man who stood for corruption and the incitement of weak and vulnerable people for his own gain. The coercion Jack had used to entrap susceptible people to commit crimes on his behalf was growing, and the vulnerability of his subjects was dangerously at risk. Customers with gambling and increasing debts were the first to be ensnared. There was no escape for them once they had carried out the crimes. He had all the evidence he needed to keep them on his payroll.

Jack's demons seemed to be everywhere when he was high and hallucinating. His paranoia was worsening, and his decisions were becoming more reckless. His first hit of Heroin had cost him a significant deal that would have taken him and his club to the next level of fame and fortune. However, he had been too preoccupied with a woman who knew how to distract a man, and he had lost the deal.

The reality was that Jack was no longer the young, dynamic man who lived under the shadow of his father, Big Jack. Once his father had taken a back seat due to age and illness, the club quickly lost the control it once had. Jack lacked his father's business acumen and was too used to everything running like clockwork to realise that someone clever was controlling the clock.

Heroin had become Jack's coping mechanism to numb himself from the complex emotions and decisions he needed to face as he struggled to run the club and its associated businesses. The drastic highs and lows were now commonplace. Jack was

THE PRICE OF SIMPLICITY

dependent on the feeling of being high, which provided a temporary escape from the pain he was trying to avoid.

When he was high, Jack felt he was on top of the world, floating away from the painful reality. However, the negative, competitive thoughts tortured him when the high wore off, affecting his relationships, sex life, love, and affection. His debts were mounting, and the feelings of desperation were intensifying. Jack was trapped in a downward spiral and didn't know how to break free.

Jack had met Patrick at a church out of town, and unknown to them both, he had wanted to tell Patrick about the very vivid and frightening episodes. Jack didn't want to confess anything in the club. He was paranoid that there were listening devices everywhere to scupper his deals, and that was the cause of his downfall.

Patrick knew addiction and mental health issues often overlap, Jack was most likely living with depression and also experiencing the high of a manic episode phase as well, and this would explain a lot.

When Jack started talking, he told Patrick of a recent incident that he was ashamed of, and it made him realise he needed help of some sort. He was not sure whether that was divine intervention or some other kind, but he thought confessing to a priest was a good start.

Jack began his story. "Two weeks ago, things were going terribly at the club, and I had gone into the back office to ease the pain. A delivery man I have known for years knocked on the office door to ask me to sign for the goods he had just delivered."

Jack continued, "When he came to the office, I saw him holding a couple of rats snapping and snarling towards me. Drool was hanging from their ravenous jaws, and their teeth were long, sharp and glistening with thick mucus. He kept holding them out towards me, and I lost the plot. I was screaming at him to get the fucking things away from me. He acted like he didn't know what I was talking about, and I couldn't get him to stop coming closer and closer with the rats held out to me. I grabbed a knife that was on the desk and stabbed him over and over. The rats jumped from his arms towards my face, and I was stabbing wildly in the air to try and kill them. The noise was unbearable, and suddenly the door burst open, and a couple of the boys dragged Reggie out screaming, blood everywhere. Then when I looked again, the rats had gone. All that was left was the knife covered in blood. Reggie was rushed to the hospital, and it was touch-and-go for a while, but they saved his life, not his eye. It had all been one big, fucking hallucination and not the first either."

Patrick was disturbed by this and asked what the man had been doing. Jack told him he was holding a receipt for me to sign and nothing more. "Of course, I compensated him for his eye, but it really scared me that I could not tell the difference between a piece of paper and a rabid rat."

Patrick could see from what Jack said that he had no remorse for his actions, only fear for his sanity. He would not offer absolution to a man who shows no remorse. Patrick needed to believe that Jack would make reasonable efforts to avoid the sin in the future, and Patrick was convinced otherwise. So he just turned and said to Jack, "I will help you fight your demons, Jack, if you join me in the fight. But, I cannot nor will not fight the demons for you."

THE PRICE OF SIMPLICITY

Jack nodded ascent, knowing Patrick's words were honest and justified. Still, at least he had said the words out loud and made an attempt at confession, which made Jack feel easier. He reflected on other events that had occurred recently that he now realised were the effects of the drugs.

A couple of weeks earlier, Jack had taken a shot of the Heroin that was becoming an increasingly more frequent habit. He had been with a woman and had used the drug to enhance the experience. Still, instead of feeling more aroused sexually, Jack became more agitated in his mood. He suddenly became angry with the woman shouting at her for his failure to perform. Jack knew it was not her fault. She was young and beautiful and paid to please men. The girl had worked hard to placate Jack and seduce him, but he had become rough, pushing her away and slapping her a few times. She was crying, and as he stood up to go to the bathroom, the floor appeared to rise and fall like an ocean. Try as he might, he just couldn't walk without falling over. His need to urinate was becoming desperate, but he couldn't move forwards or backwards. He lay on the floor and tried to roll towards the bucket he kept for the night-time. But each time he got to it, the bucket moved away. Grabbing at the bucket now in desperation, it spilt the contents onto the floor, and Jack urinated where he lay. The girl had grabbed her clothes and fled, no doubt to tell all and sundry about what had just happened, that Jack was losing control of everything, not just the business.

A few days after this first incident, Jack had been in his car, and without warning, the wheel had grown in his hands. He had tried to crush it back to its original size, but nothing happened. Jack was frantically trying to steer the car, and it kept on growing and shrinking. Ultimately, he had to pull over and wait until the episode had passed. He checked the wheel later but could find no fault in it.

Then last weekend, he had been laid on the settee as the euphoria swept through his body from the Heroin when he noticed what looked like beetles crawling all over the walls. He cursed, thinking there must be a nest and he would deal with it in the morning. Then it was as if the walls were moving as the mass of beetles became dense. It made his skin crawl watching them. They were running up and down over each other. Some bit the heads of others, and he could see streaks of blood on the wall from the headless corpses. He had felt himself gasping and drawing his legs under him as the stream ran across the carpet. Throwing whatever he could grab onto the writhing heap of insects didn't deter them. Onwards they came, he heard himself shouting for help, and when the door opened and daylight flooded in, he looked to see they had all disappeared.

Jack knew he had to stop this habit, but it was more complex than he had imagined. He had always looked down on addicts thinking they were weak and lacked the strength of mind and body. Jack had believed in the past if addicts didn't quit, it was because they didn't want to, not because they couldn't. And now, he was fighting the same demons as the low life he had despised all his adult life.

Whether it was the drugs, the dept or sheer desperation, when Jack heard on the grapevine that there was a lot of money to be gained by supplying the right kind of girl to a select clientele, he saw his chance to escape from this rat race. He put all the drugs, debts and ill feelings behind him. Jack would take one of his current lovers or go alone and find a new mistress somewhere warmer than bloody Huddersfield. He would leave his frigid wife and the son he had never bothered to get to know behind and start a new and happy life without demons or moving wallpaper. This spurred Jack to discover as much as he could about the supply and demand of a precious commodity he felt he could source.

All the debts that Jack had were intrinsically linked back to Bill Black, not all directly, but he was the source of every penny he owed. He would die happy if he could get that particular monkey off his back. So, Jack followed his nose to the ones spreading the word about the new merchandise being sought. They were precise about what kind of girls they wanted; anything less would not even be considered. From the description he had been given, he had just the person in mind and got word back to the people putting out feelers that he could supply what they wanted and at short notice.

Jack had at least felt vindicated after his confession, and once he left Patrick, he was determined to clinch the deal and move on.

Patrick realised for the first time that even a man addicted to drugs had the sense to realise he was not a tree; he could uproot and move on. Now Patrick needed to face the life that had been forced upon him. He was down, but he was not out. In his head, he said, "Welcome back, Patrick."

LEARNING THE SYSTEM

Patrick had been taken to Wakefield Prison, or the 'Monster Mansion' as many people had dubbed it, for the sheer number of high-profile, high-risk sex offenders and murderers.

Ironically it is situated on 'Love Lane', but love is not what you see as you step down from the prison van and into the yard. The cold, bleak, four-storey building plagued Patrick as he was ushered inside. Thoughts bounced around his head and made him question everything. "If only he had stayed in Spain." "If only he hadn't seen the papers in Jack's office." "If only he had stayed and made love to Elizabeth and let the police handle everything." Outside his cell door, the stark metal railings along the corridor guarded the drop below. Many end up over the railings either by force or as a quicker way out of their sentence, unable to withstand the pressure any longer. Death is chosen as the only imagined escape route.

But he hadn't, and now he had to face up to the fact that this was his new life. He would have to learn to live with the consequences and readjust to conform to prison life. The first decision he needed to make was whether he should present as a priest or a murderer? Patrick knew the guards and prison authorities would treat him like everyone else regardless of whether he appeared as a priest or ex-priest. But, his faith was something he felt strongly about. To survive in this institution,

THE PRICE OF SIMPLICITY

he would need all the advantages he could get to stay alive and endure a life amongst rapists and murderers.

Patrick's biggest fear was that he would be gang-raped again, and he would do anything to avoid this happening. Prisons were notoriously famed for sexual violence and knew no jurisdictional boundaries concerning prisoner rapes. Patrick needed to find a protector quickly before becoming the gang's prey. If God acted as his protector, he would need to be the priest and gather a flock to safeguard him from the ever-circling sharks that permeate prison life.

Patrick had to use his brain, experience, education and contacts to ensure his safety. As he endured the humiliating strip search and all his personal belongings were taken, he requested that he keep his dog collar. After thoroughly inspecting it for hidden blades and other contraband, he was allowed to take it inside with him. Patrick noticed that one of the guards on his wing wore a crucifix and made a mental note to form a relationship with the guard as soon as he was settled. He knew he would need to be a cold-blooded manipulator and exploit others or become a victim of the system he had to live in for the unforeseeable future. Manipulation or "the name of the game" is expected. Only a naïve person would start prison life guilefully telling the truth and trusting others.

After the rough and wretched first night was over and his door was unlocked, he left the isolation of his solitary cell to join the prison population. He would be allocated a shared cell that day and requested it to be a Catholic or Christian. After slopping out, the prisoners were led into the canteen for the day's first meal. Patrick knew not to demonstrate any weakness but wore his dog collar regardless. He needed it to be understood that he was a priest. He hoped there were enough high-ranking Catholic criminals inside to be noticed as an asset rather than a weak link to the outside world. But trust, even for a priest, has to be earned, and it was only a short time before his endeavours to save the world got noticed.

Patrick's request for a Catholic cellmate was granted a few days later when a new arrival was given the same cell. Patrick was unaware of his crimes but had heard the jeers from the other inmates when the man was led on the corridor to the cell. His partnership with the priest had been orchestrated to segregate them from the main prison population. The idea was to keep them both locked in for most of the day to stop the expected violent attacks on his cellmate. The governing bodies imagined Patrick as a priest, would be more tolerant of the man than most other inmates.

As soon as the man was shown into the cell, Patrick's hackles automatically rose. He felt like a snake had slithered over his body as he shuddered in the repulsion of the man before him. The man held out his hand, but Patrick would not take it. Instead, Patrick indicated that the man took the lower bunk and he climbed atop the upper bunk. Patrick watched as the man laid out his belongings, occasionally turning to sneer at Patrick, whose face showed no softness. The man was trying to gauge Patrick for weaknesses and, seeing his dog collar decided he must have fragilities he could manipulate.

When all the man's belongings had been laid on the table and window ledge, he turned up to Patrick, introduced himself as Ben Laker, and said to the priest before him. "I might need your confessional services, Father. I have a lot of stories that you might find entertaining, given that you are a priest. Perhaps we could share some stories over the long days ahead."

As he spoke, Patrick noticed he was rubbing himself in arousal, and this disturbed Patrick immensely. Patrick wondered. "Did the man think he was a homosexual because he was a priest, or was there some other reason this man Ben Laker, was acting like they were kindred spirits?"

THE PRICE OF SIMPLICITY

Patrick realised as he lay on his bunk locked down with this heinous man that the prisoners would soon believe they were of the same ilk, and reprisals would be brought down on both men. Patrick didn't yet know the man's crimes. All he knew so far was his reputation had proceeded him, and now they were both in danger. Patrick had to find a way to escape the cell he shared with this man.

When they had been unlocked for lunch, they were spat upon and taunted as the cellmates made their way to the canteen and back again as if they were one. The atmosphere was charged, and it was only a matter of time before one of them was attacked; Patrick needed to ensure it was not him. Patrick did his best to distance himself from his cellmate, but it was difficult in the confines of the block.

Patrick took one of the screws aside and beseeched him to get an appointment with the Governor to discuss his new cellmate. "I can't promise that the Governor will see you, but I will advise you. Your new cellmate Ben Laker likes to kill, and if he gets the chance, he will kill you, so sleep with one eye open if you can. The only way he will ever leave the 'Monster Mansion' is in a coffin."

Patrick didn't fear death so much as being unable to stop anyone from touching him sexually, worse still, raping him. He could not prevent this instilled fear from becoming totally irrational. He would kill before he was raped again. Along with being raped was his fear of responding to another man's touch. He found he could not breathe when Patrick even considered the possibility of Ben or anyone like him putting him into a position where he was helpless to stop them from performing perverted acts on him. Patrick started to have a panic attack and had to work hard to steady himself enough to return to the cell. Never would he allow that to happen to him again. He would take a life to protect himself; he was even prepared to take his own life to stop what he considered the vilest act ever.

Later that afternoon, locked inside the cell, Ben began to talk about his crimes with obvious relish. They were sick crimes against runaway boys, and Patrick seethed with fury and disgust. Patrick warned Ben to stop, but he would not heed the warning; this spurred him on more. Ben paused as the door was unlocked for the evening, and an officer put his head around the door to tell them to line up.

When the officer disappeared, Ben continued to talk and masturbate, talking about a young boy he had tortured, describing the boy's screams in detail. Patrick jumped off his bunk and, grabbing Ben, pulled him from his cot and demanded that Ben shut up. Patrick threw him onto the ground kicking him; Ben reached up and took hold of Patrick's testicles, grinning up at him, blood trickling out of the corner of his mouth. Patrick began to panic, searching for anything to smash this man's head in and make him release his grip. When all he got was a pen off the table, with all his strength, he drove it as deep and as hard as he could into Ben's ear. Patrick was aware of nothing, only survival from the sensation of drowning and being unable to breathe. Ben's grip fell away, and something caught his attention as Patrick looked down at the dying man before him. He raised his eyes to the door to see a man looking in at what he had just done. The man didn't speak; he just turned and walked on.

Patrick was shocked and afraid by what he had just done; he wanted to be sick as he looked down at the man at his feet. Patrick could clearly see a wet stain in Ben's trousers, and unsure if it was urine or seamen, Patrick shuddered his revulsion. He walked quickly from the cell and followed the others to the canteen. A few men jeered at him and taunted him, but it was less than usual as his cellmate Ben was not with him. He lined up and got his food but couldn't eat it; he was visibly shaking and looked ill, his hands and face sweating from the exertion

THE PRICE OF SIMPLICITY

he had just applied to his dying or dead cellmate. Patrick sat with his head down until he was tapped on the shoulder, and he was told to go and join another table that seated four of the hardened criminals on the wing. One of the men indicated to a chair, and Patrick sat down nervously. Nobody said anything to him throughout lunch, and thoughts of what he had just done swirling about in his head and the anxiety he felt at this table made the sickness inside almost unbearable. The other prisoners looked on, wondering if this would be a reprisal. Even the guards were watching and waiting for something to happen.

At the end of the meal, one of the men whispered in his ear to follow them, which he did, wondering if this was when he would be beaten, raped or even murdered. Patrick followed the men inside the cell, and the door was closed. The guy Patrick knew to be the highest-ranking sat on a chair, and the others stood around. The silence was deafening before the seated man said, "What was that all about?"

Patrick paused, wondering what he should say; he knew this powerful man was talking about the murder he had just committed but was at a loss just how much to disclose. He chose to tell the truth as the murder had all but been witnessed anyway. "I was locked in my cell without consent with a man who enjoyed relating his crimes to me. When he spoke of the abuse of young and vulnerable boys, I told him to stop. When he wouldn't stop, I decided to silence him permanently."

Patrick took a deep breath and continued, "As you know, I am a man of God, but even God has his limits. I know my sins were witnessed, but all our sins are seen before God, and if I have penance to pay, I will accept that punishment. The question is, are you the one who will punish me or am I to atone to my God?"

The man looked at length at Patrick as his fingertips formed a bridge in front of his body before he clasped his hands together. "Oh, I think I should be thanking this priest that saves me a

SHELAGH TAYLOR

job. The man was set to die today either way and if we hadn't witnessed your disgust at the man, then your life would have ended too."

Patrick's relief was audible as he let out a long sigh of gratitude; his legs almost gave way, and he had to be helped to sit by one of the men, watching and waiting. "During our evening meal, I was told a few facts about you, Patrick Herron. I was sure you were a priest like many others I knew in my childhood, especially when I saw you up and down with the paedophile and locked up with him all day. I made the assumption you were both the same and that you were guilty of taking the underage girl to sell for sex. But from what I have heard on the streets, what wasn't revealed in court is that you were true to your word when you said you were saving her. Yet, you never gave anyone's name that might speak up for you. You took your punishment, and I suppose you trusted your God to help you."

Patrick replied that the story was primarily true, and although he was a priest, he was not without sin. Although never a sin to a child or vulnerable person.

"I may have a use for you, Father Herron; as you may or may not know, we are a strong Catholic family from across the sea in Ireland. We, too, are not without sin, and it would help our Mammie back home to know we had our own priest in residence until we have finished our sentence. I also have a brother in this prison, and if you agree to be our priest, you can be assured of life here free from harm."

Patrick nodded as the man continued, "The little job you did for me earlier will not be seen as a murder '<u>YOU</u> 'committed. Somebody in the Governor's office already admitted to the crime you did <u>NOT</u> witness nor were you aware of. Now go back to your cell and be amazed your cellmate is gone."

The door was opened for Patrick, and he made his way back

to his cell, thanking God that he had found his protector, the very scary and infamous Kieran Delaney and his brother Chester Delaney.

VISITING ORDER

As soon as Elizabeth read the postmark, she knew who had sent the letter, but didn't have time to open it, so she hastily pushed it into her work bag and waved goodbye to the children. She made her way to work, anxious to get some privacy to open and read the letter lying and beckoning to her from her bag. Elizabeth slammed her clock card into the machine and turned towards the steps. As she reached the first floor and turned the corner, ready to climb to the next level, Robert was waiting and caught her arm. She roughly shrugged his hand off her arm and raised her chin into the air in the act of a defiant snub strode on. Robert begged. "Elizabeth, please listen to me. I didn't mean to hurt you. It meant nothing; Beryl is hardly in your class. I just felt so frustrated when I got back from Blackpool. I had thought it would be a wonderfully romantic weekend with the children, and we would sleep together and make love. I felt hurt when you put up the usual barriers and didn't want to spend time alone with me. I was confused."

"I cannot believe that you are trying to blame me for your lack of restraint. You purposely went to seek Beryl out with the full intention of bedding her, knowing her reputation. Well, lucky for you, there were no barriers in sight with her. God knows what diseases she carries around, sleeping with one and all like she does. Oh, and by the way, she wanted to blow you as well, apparently. Last week I had no idea what that meant, but I am fully aware now, Robert. I hope you got everything you wanted and more besides."

THE PRICE OF SIMPLICITY

Elizabeth had started to walk away but turned back to say, "I was falling for you, and I had hoped our children would become 'OUR family', but thankfully I found out what the 'REAL' Robert is like before it was too late and we were married." Elizabeth turned and stomped off with tears in her eyes, but at least she had said her piece, and now she was too late to go to the bathroom the read the letter in her bag. She would have to wait until break time and pray it would be good news for a change.

Molly was surprised when she saw Elizabeth come around the corner. She had expected to either take the day off or come in all red-eyed and weepy. But, she seemed to be bearing up. Molly thought, "Good for her."

As they began to work deeply in thought, both women thought about the future, and both were uncertain about what it had to offer. At the first break, Elizabeth asked Molly if she would mind if they sat at their tables for the morning break and not join the other women. "I can't face that bloody cow today, Molly. I could swing for her as she deliberately played her cards to get Robert. Well, bloody good luck to them both. Robert has proved his worth to me, and I know now he can't be trusted. I am devasted, but at least I hadn't gotten married or, worse, still gotten pregnant with him. His life is his own, and I must look to my future. I am not getting any younger, and I need to start looking for a better, kinder, more faithful man to make me happy. Do you want to join me, Molly, in my search?"

When Molly said a resounding 'YES', Elizabeth was amazed, "Really, Molly, do you want to help me find another man? We could look together, Molly, for two rich and handsome men?" Both women laughed.

A few days later, Molly was animated and said she had seen and had cut out an ad in the Examiner, asking for single people to come along and join in the fun at Huddersfield's first Singles

Club,' THE PHOENIX'. When Molly and Elizabeth read the advert together, they were instantly excited that they might find true love and happiness. It would be held every Friday night in the town centre above the Zetland Pub. The women were excited to go to a place where everyone would be single and in the same boat as them. With all the talk about joining the Phoenix Club, finding a regular babysitter and finding the man of their dreams, the letter in Elizabeth's bag remained unread. Just as the break ended, she thought about it, but it was too late. She would have to wait until the lunchtime break.

Elizabeth raced to the toilet at lunchtime with the letter hidden inside her pocket. Once inside the cubicle, she took the note and opened the envelope. Inside was a 'Visiting Order' that invited Elizabeth to visit with Patrick Gregory Herron on the fifteenth of November at Her Majesty's Prison Wakefield, West Yorkshire, at two in the afternoon. She was to take two forms of ID with her and arrive at least one hour before the visiting time for processing.

As Elizabeth read the order, she held it away. She gasped as if it was a dangerous item that could be detonated. She was frozen in position, eyes wide and an incredulous look staring at the paper. Elizabeth looked from left to right, above her and below, to check that no one else was privy to the letter. It was the first time in her life that she had been invited to visit a prison, and the thought petrified her.

Elizabeth had just four weeks to decide if it was the right thing to do. If only she had someone she could talk to about Patrick.... Could she face Patrick behind bars and tell him she would not wait for him. Harangue him for abandoning her and going against her wishes, berate him for killing her uncle, accuse him of not loving her enough...

LIFE INSIDE HER PRISON

Patrick was now part of the notorious 'Delaney Gang'; he had yet to earn any status. His worth would be decided over time, and the Delaney's planned to utilise the most expedient and practical benefits of a 'Puppet Priest' in the prison system.

If they could not find a practical use for him, he would be removed as a worthless asset to them. It was in Patrick's best interest to prove his worth and engage in ideas that would benefit the Delaney's and make him indispensable.

Patrick came up with the idea that prison chaplains could visit the cells of other cons and encourage them to live a more Christian, crime-free life. Once he gained the trust of the governing bodies, then the Delaney's would be able to up the ante, and this avenue would be used to distribute goods throughout the prison. But, first, the Delaney brothers would need to ensure that Patrick was recognised as the priest everyone wanted to worship with, confess to and take Christian lessons from. Therefore, teaching the prison population to live free of crime and retribution and helping the Governor run a more respectable prison even as it became increasingly overcrowded.

Kieran Delaney thought this was a brilliant idea and was pleased that Patrick had shown himself as an innovative conceptualist who could take ideas and improve on them. Patrick was proving himself to be of worth. If he continued, he would be an asset to their corporation and rise up the tiers of his fictive kin.

Patrick needed to be tested, and his first task was to establish himself as a leader of the prison chapel so that he would become an obvious choice as a pastoral leader when the current Chaplain met with a fatal accident.

Patrick articulated that it would work if he showed that he had converted Chester Delaney to turn the other cheek and be more forgiving. He would need Chester to take his Christian beliefs seriously and turn to God instead of crimes. Patrick would need to set up a place of worship where the gang members could come to talk or confess that was in confidence. If this was seen to work, the Governors might be convinced that Patrick was the man for the job. Kieran and Chester howled with laughter when Patrick fed them this idea but understood it would only be short-term and would benefit them; they agreed to give it a go and spoke to one of the screws on their payroll to organise a room that Patrick could use as a chapel. They made it known that the prisoners did not trust the current Chaplain with their confessions and needed a man like Patrick, whom they trusted to be their link to God.

Patrick would need to start preaching to a group of men who would grow more extensive and more avid in their following over the coming weeks. They would then need to stage something, perhaps an incident where Chester would have the opportunity to forgive his offender and turn the other cheek. Maybe he could quote some passages from the bible for effect. When word got back to the Governor, he would start asking questions. Once the Chaplain had his accident, Patrick would be instated into the role of prison Chaplin. Patrick advised the Delaney's that this scheme would take time; they had to trust him to get the job done and build the trust needed.

The business could flourish and expand once Patrick ordered the new candles, bibles, crucifixes, etc. For now, they had to play it cool. It had already been noted that Patrick, an ordained priest, had joined their group, and now he needed to show he was trying hard to guide them. It was a start, and they would have to play the game if the scheme was going to work.

Thankfully for Patrick, after the death of Ben Laker, the top bunk was taken out of his cell, and it once again became the single cell it was designed to be. The influence of the Delaney's had a part in this, and Patrick quickly realised the power this family held even in prison.

Patrick had been given his first task, and it was also a test. It was arranged that he would hear the confession of one of the prisoners in line for a beating for a minor offence against the rules of the Delaney's. It was organised that Patrick would be in a cell. The repentant man would be giving his confession when another prisoner would burst in and start beating the man. Patrick would stop the beating by reminding him of forgiveness. The offending prisoner would then stop and think about it. He would then ask the man he was beating to forgive him. Of course, the man would be taken off to the hospital to be dealt with whilst Patrick atoned the offending prisoner so he could receive forgiveness.

The Delaney's found these scenarios hilarious and treated it like a game choosing people to be beaten in front of Patrick and then dropping to their knees, suddenly seeing the error of their ways. Patrick reminded them it would never work if they took the proverbial piss out of the scheme. The authorities would see straight through the scam and put a stop to it before it even got started. Patrick felt like he was dealing with errant boys instead of men that had killed, the way they laughed and slapped their thighs whenever they thought up another bizarre set-up. Patrick knew if these scams failed to work, he would be redundant and at the mercy of the prison system. He was done for without the protection of the Delaney's; a wolf was always hovering to pick off the weak and vulnerable prisoners to turn into their sex slaves. The Delaney's were predators too, but they used their prey to do favours, like moving contraband that was the prison currency in exchange for protection.

Patrick left the Delaney cell to find the Chaplain and begin his part of the deal. He could hear the Delaney brothers laughing all the way down the wing corridor, the laughter rebounding off the metal walls and ceiling making it sound even more sinister. The violence and power the two brothers were notorious for disturbed Patrick; he was aware that he was aiding and abetting known gangsters, yet in a way, their crimes aligned with his own.

They had been arrested and later sentenced for the death of nine men and four women involved in people trafficking. With other gangs, the Delaney brothers ran most of Liverpool's underworld. When drugs became the primary earner of British cities, people trafficking soon followed. Although the Delaney's had a part in the supply and demand of class-A drugs, loan sharking and debt collection, they drew the line regarding buying and selling vulnerable people.

The brothers knew the more desperate a person was, the easier they were to convince them to sell their children for forced labour and, in some cases, sexual slavery, especially when the demand for younger victims became a significant part of the deals.

Other gangs associated with the syndicate, the Delaney, were part of voted to join this lucrative endeavour. Still, the Delaney's refused to be a part of it and stood fast. They knew traffickers looked for individuals who were feeling hopeless or struggling with dependency.

THE PRICE OF SIMPLICITY

The Delaney's knew many of their customers had been targeted due to their desperation over debts they couldn't pay and a desperate need to get out of the rut they had put themselves in. These desperate individuals had been approached and offered considerable money in exchange for their son or daughter coming to work for the syndicate. They were told that the child would have to work complicated cleaning and doing jobs around their clients' houses until their debts were cleared; in other words, they were slave labour. What they didn't tell the drug or gambling addicts was that some of them would be forced into sexual slavery, too, with no hope of escape.

When Kieran and Chester Delaney heard their name had been linked with the kidnapping, rape and murder of children, they were furious and set about a vigilante mission to kill those responsible and free them. They knew they were going against more muscular and considerable opposition than they could handle. Still, the cruelty of children gnawed at them so much they went in all guns blazing.

Every police officer on their payroll was alerted to the underworld's dealings with child trafficking and told that if they didn't act quickly to apprehend the people responsibly, the Delaney's would personally take them down. What had surprised Kieran and Chester was that women were involved in this vile and despicable endeavour. They could not comprehend any woman with maternal instincts could possibly bring themselves to acknowledge and allow this type of crime to be committed and help with it.

When the Delaney's found the people responsible for trading these children, they planned an operation to take them in a swoop and bring them to a storage unit for questioning. This all happened within hours of the police being informed, and Kieran and Chester set about extracting information from each of these abhorrent men and women. If they didn't freely give information, they were tortured until they did. Everyone suffered beyond belief with methods no ordinary person could or would ever use.

When they had sufficient information to give to the police about the whereabouts of many of these victims, then this was quickly passed on to the police. When they had finished with the people responsible, the police were given the address of the storage unit where they could find the beaten, battered, burnt and brutalised remains.

Shortly after, Kieran and Chester were arrested and sentenced to life in HMP Wakefield.

When Patrick heard the story behind the arrest of the Delaney brothers, he felt empathy towards the men. Even though he knew they had been responsible for the brutalisation of men and women to some degree, he condoned their actions, knowing he had done the same. Patrick didn't feel quite so dirty working for the men any longer. He thought this would be an excellent time to contact Elizabeth and see if she would come and visit him. Patrick needed to explain so much to her. As he found the Chaplin, he passed one of the officers he knew who worked with the Delaney boys and requested a visiting order.

OWEN'S REVELATION

Margaret missed her sister, Vera, it seemed like everyone was beginning a new life, and she was stuck in the past, afraid of the future. Margaret decided to travel to Scarborough to visit Vera and meet Owen, the man her sister had on a pedestal. She wrote a letter to Vera asking if it was convenient to come and stay for a long weekend sometime in mid-November.

Margaret explained that the doctor had arranged an appointment with her for the first week in November but would be accessible until later when she was to see the optician. Just writing the letter to Vera made Margaret feel happier. She loved Elizabeth and the children, but it was not the same as chatting with your sister and sharing familiar life changes. Margaret had a spring in her step as she walked onto the post box and posted the letter. She secretly hoped that Owen may have had a friend so the four of them could go out and have a laugh. It was such a long time since she had acted like a woman instead of a mother or nanna; Margaret hoped this might be the turning point she needed in her life.

It was a wonderful surprise when, less than a week later, Vera replied that she would love Margaret to come and stay with her. Vera added that Friday the thirteenth of November until Sunday the fifteenth would be ideal as she could get tickets for the pantomime Aladdin at the Scarborough Theatre.

When Elizabeth finished work that day, the visiting order was still lying in the bottom of her work bag so she could look at it each day while deciding what to do. As soon as she opened the door, her mother announced, "You will never guess; I have booked the bus to Scarborough to see Vera. I will spend Friday, Saturday and most of Sunday with her and return late on Sunday night. I am so excited; I can't remember the last time I went anywhere alone. I feel like a teenager going on my first holiday. So, if you have any plans for that weekend, I won't be around to babysit. Margaret's smile spread across her face and lit up her eyes, something Elizabeth hadn't seen in a long time.

Margaret's news finalised Elizabeth's thoughts about visiting Patrick and made the decision for her. It was now impossible to go and see him without the children, and she wasn't about to subject her children to a prison visit. Now that she had the address she needed, she would write him a letter instead and wait and see what came of that. She felt relieved she wasn't comfortable visiting a prison, and now she had no choice. It seemed more manageable.

Margaret hadn't stopped talking about going away since she had received the reply from Vera that morning. The children had assumed they would be going too and were disappointed when she told them otherwise. So Margaret had promised to bring Maggie and Lizzie something back from her weekend away. As far as she was concerned, this earned her the right to continue to talk about it. The children were only interested in what she was going to bring them. They were not interested in how long it was since their nanna had been on holiday alone or how long it was since she had seen her sister. Maggie and Lizzie imagined it would be boring going to the seaside as an adult; you were too big for a donkey ride or to build sandcastles, so what on earth would you do all day?

Elizabeth was glad for her mum; it would give her and Vera a chance to talk about Jack together and reminisce about their childhood antics and also an opportunity to grieve together.

Although Vera had never been as close to Jack as Margaret, he had still been her brother, and, therefore, she also mourned his violent death.

The bus pulled into Scarborough bus station, and Vera stood waiting to meet her sister. It was months since they had seen each other, and although they never hugged or talked soppy to each other, the bond between them was apparent. Vera had brought Owen to take them back in his car to Vera's two-bedroom flat. Margaret was grateful for the lift; she was tired from her journey and graciously accepted Owen's help with her case. When she sat back in the car, she realised there were embroidered cushions along the back window and other feminine touches that surprised her for a single man on his own to consider. Margaret surmised that maybe he had an elderly mother he took out in the car; she did not think Vera would have asked for it.

Owen seemed friendly and chatted amicably on the journey back. Once they got to Vera's flat, Margaret was shown her room, and they all sat down to a cup of tea. Owen said he had a few jobs and would have to go soon but would see both the following day to take them to the theatre. As they chatted, Margaret asked him various questions to get to know him and gauge his suitability and trustworthiness if Owen was going to be a part of their family. He seemed cagey about where he lived and what had happened to his wife; Owen just said he was a widow and didn't want to discuss it. Owen seemed reluctant to elaborate on the life he shared with his wife, and Margaret decided he must still find it hard to talk about her. Once Owen had gone, Vera and Margaret could speak openly. Margaret asked Vera if she had ever been to his house or if she knew anything more about Owen. Vera admitted that he avoided taking her home and talking about his life, sometimes making her suspicious. Still, she was so happy with him that she put it back in her mind.

As the evening progressed, Vera and Margaret began to recollect when they had both worked at Wellington Mills and talked about the mill trips they used to have to Blackpool every year. "We had such fun in those days; everything made us laugh. We were so young and carefree, even though we had both had our share of troubles." Reflected Vera.

Margaret said, "Do you remember the year Brenda Whitham got caught having a wee behind one of the buses parked up on the spare land. She had looked all around and was assured no one could see her, then hid behind what she thought was a redundant bus. When it drove off, she was there with her bare backside stuck in the air as the tram passed, everyone looking and waving. She always thought she was somebody until that happened."

"Was that the year Colin had returned to the bus drunk and, as it was locked, laid underneath it out of the cold and fell asleep. When everybody returned to the bus, he was missing, and we decided to leave him, and the bus drove off. Luckily it didn't run over him, but it woke him up. He jumped up, shouting and waving his arms as the bus drove away without anybody noticing him. I remember he was furious on Monday. He had to buy a train ticket and then walk home from Huddersfield Railway station to Marsh." Vera recalled.

"What about when we all sat in that working man's club on the front, and Henry Bowler was kissing Peggy and acting like the goat."

Margaret said, "I remember she jumped on his knee, and the stool collapsed, and they both fell backwards and through the fire door out onto the Promenade."

Vera added, "I remember her legs stuck up in the air and the tatty knickers she was wearing left nothing to the imagination."

THE PRICE OF SIMPLICITY

Both women laughed until tears rolled down their cheeks. "If only life was so simple now, I feel old before my time and have no life of my own anymore. I feel fat, fifty and fed up. I don't suppose Owen has any nice friends we could pal up with for tomorrow's night trip to the theatre?" asked Margaret.

Vera retorted, "You are nearer sixty than fifty, Margaret, and Owen has never mentioned any friends, single or otherwise. I'm afraid he plays his cards very close to his chest."
"Never mind, Vera, it was just a thought."

The women talked late into the night before they decided to make a cup of cocoa and go to bed. They would go into Scarborough the next day, and Margaret would get a present each for the girls. "Just get them a stick of rock each Margaret, you spend far too much money on them kids, and they don't appreciate it." Chided Vera.

For once, Margaret agreed money was tight, and it had cost her an arm and a leg, with the bus fares and theatre tickets, on top. It had taken all the spare money she had this week. Margaret had to wait until Thursday before her next wage was payable. Working part-time had taken its toll on any money left over by the time payday came around again. But she couldn't work full time and be there for the children when they came home from school each day, so she thought it was worth it. But if prices continued to rise, she would have to return full-time until she retired in two years. Margaret worried about how she was going to manage the pension. As for the children, they would just have to hang about outside the mill until their mother finished work. Margaret was sure Samuel Martin would let the children wait inside by the clock machine; if it was raining. It was only for an hour, but that was a worry for another time.

Vera washed and made breakfast Saturday morning when Margaret entered the kitchen. "You're up early, Vera. You never

SHELAGH TAYLOR

used to back home."

"I seem to have gotten used to getting up early whilst I have been seeing Owen, he usually has to dash off when he stays over, and it just got to be a habit." Replied Vera.

"What did you say he did for a living Vera?"

"Travelling salesman, he sells insurance and seems to have his fingers in many pies. It was him that got me this flat to rent. He collects rent too. That's how I first met him. He collects for a firm in Huddersfield, and he had called into the Wellington pub one Friday night when I was there, and we just got chatting. He told me he had a caravan near Scarborough and asked me if I would like to go and stay in it one weekend. That was it. After that first weekend, I was smitten."

Margaret jumped in. "You mean you didn't even know him when you went to stay in his caravan? Oh, Vera, you are such a foolish woman. He could have been a mass murderer."
Vera jumped back, "You mean like that priest your Elizabeth knows. Just because you know somebody doesn't mean you can trust them. You should know that; just look at Charles."

Margaret was shocked to hear Vera be so defensive of Owen and nasty about her and Charles. She didn't care about that bloody priest; she couldn't agree more. There was an awkward silence, and Margaret went to get washed and dressed. She didn't want there to be an atmosphere on this rare weekend away. Margaret would say something nice about Owen and hope Vera forgave her.

The two women had a lovely time in Scarborough visiting 'Peasholme Park', a favourite of them both. At lunch on the seafront, Margaret bought the two sticks of rock as she had agreed. Then it was time to head home to get ready for the theatre. Margaret was excited. Ken Dodd was the last time she

THE PRICE OF SIMPLICITY

had been at the theatre, and when she reminded Vera about that night, they both laughed about it.

Owen picked them up at six as arranged, and the women told him about their day. Margaret asked what he had done, but he skirted around the question and talked about the football scores.

When they entered the theatre, they got their tickets and enjoyed the performance's first half immensely. In the interval, Vera and Margaret wanted ice cream, and Owen said he would stay in the seats and watch their bags whilst they went and got one. They had to queue for a while, and by the time they had been to the toilet, it was time to return to their seats. Owen ducked out to the bathroom just as the lights went out.

After the show, they heard someone shouting Owen's name as they exited. He did his best to hurry them on, but Margaret stopped him and said, "Owen, someone is shouting for you."

The pause was needed for the stranger and his wife to catch up to them. The man smiled broadly and said, "Owen, I thought it was you. Where's Lucy? Are you going to introduce us to your friends?"

Owen began to stutter and look embarrassed. The man repeated, "Where's Lucy Owen?"

He turned towards Margaret and Vera and explained, "Hello ladies, I'm Bill, and this is my wife, Conny. We are excellent friends with Owen and his wife, Lucy. I wish we had known you were all coming to tonight's show; we could have made it a night and all come together."

Margaret and Vera looked at each other and shook the man's hand, then made an excuse to visit the bathroom, leaving Owen to explain to his friends who they were and where his wife was that evening. As soon as they were in the toilets, Margaret asked

83

Vera, "Did you know he was married, Vera?"

"No, I didn't, I swear. I occasionally had a few suspicions but dismissed them as I liked Owen so much. Honestly, I didn't want it to be true."

"Oh Vera, what are we going to do?"

Vera replied, "Please don't say anything to him, Margaret; let me deal with it in my own way. When you have gone home, I will arrange to see him and have it out with him. I need to know if it is over with his wife or what."

Owen stood alone when the pair exited the bathroom, waiting for them. Margaret didn't speak a word to him, and to give Vera her due, she was very frosty with him too. "I think you need to take us straight home; Owen and I would like to see you tomorrow night when Margaret has gone home. I think you have some explaining to do." Vera said in a severe tone.

Owen just nodded and led them out to the car; he looked like he had seen a ghost. Margaret was dying to know what he had told the couple but kept her word to Vera and didn't say anything.

Most married women feared single women like Margaret and Vera. Margaret felt sorry for Vera; she knew what it was like to live year after year as a single woman. People looked down on you as if you couldn't get her or, more importantly, keep a man for yourself.

Probably not so much now at their age, but when they were younger, desirable and better looking than most other married women. Then they turned the heads of a lot of married men, Margaret would be disgusted if a married man tried to make a pass at her, but Vera had always thought it was funny and game for a laugh. Margaret always thought about what a man is worth when he is married to someone else and prepared to cheat on

THE PRICE OF SIMPLICITY

her. It had happened to her, and she vowed she would never make anyone feel like that bloody, blonde bitch that cajoled Charles to leave his beautiful wife and child. He had chosen to make a life with a woman who needed to wear a wig because her hair was so thin. And, if it wasn't for her eyes and nose, you would never know which way her head was facing. The cheating whore had no chest or hips; she was like a pencil with a sharp face. When Margaret realised the venom she was exercising in these thoughts, she laughed, aware she was not quite over the shame of losing Charles even after all these years.

Vera and Margaret talked deep into the night about what had just happened and how Vera could deal with it. Vera had shed a few tears and spoken about how much it had hurt her to find out the truth. She needed to know the whole story before she made any final decisions. Margaret knew that Vera was clutching at straws if she hoped there would be a positive explanation. Margaret tried to tell Vera, "He's just like all men, Vera; he wants to have his cake and eat it too. Owen wants all the good bits and ignores the bad bits. If he has troubles in his marriage, he needs to sort it out with his wife, not turn to another woman for what his marriage is missing. You must think about his wife Vera and how you would feel."

"I know how I feel now, Margaret, angry and upset; please don't put me down any lower than I am already feeling."
"You are going to have to face facts though, Vera; if he is married, and doesn't intend to leave his wife any time soon, then he never will."
"I know I am being silly, Margaret, but I wish we hadn't seen that couple tonight. Then I would be no wiser and could continue enjoying Owen's company. He had meant so much to me over the past year. Our love has grown, and I was going to say trust has grown too, but now it's all ruined. Oh Margaret, whatever am I going to do? I don't want to lose him; I love him?"
"Let's sleep on it, Vera; things always seem easier in the light of

day." Margaret's voice was kind and nurturing, and Vera turned to look at her sister, giving her a woeful smile and nodded.

As Margaret and Vera went to their rooms, their earlier happiness had disappeared to be replaced with worries and concerns, heads down and thoughts far away.

Sunday was a bright and sunny day that did not match the mood of either Margaret or Vera. Margaret was saddened to leave Vera alone to cope with her heartbreak. The women moped about all day until it was time for Margaret to go. The sisters hugged and said their goodbyes, and Margaret wished Vera the best of luck as she climbed into the taxi to take her to the bus station.

WHAT HAVE YOU DONE PATRICK?

Patrick had met the Chaplain and talked to him about his years serving as a priest, first in the town of Huddersfield and then later in the mountainous regions of Spain. The Chaplain was a well-travelled man and spoke at length to Patrick about the places he had visited as a missionary he had once worked for. Similarities were discussed as both had worked in remote areas worldwide. Still, the Chaplain had often worked in hostile places where he was not welcome. They had both studied theology and whereas Patrick had learned in a seminary, the Chaplain, Father Pie, had studied theology at Wycliffe Hall, Oxford. He told Patrick, "Wycliffe Hall is the one place in Britain with worse food and plumbing than prison".

Patrick questioned Father Pie to establish if he thought he was welcome in prison and did the crimes, and the men disgust him. Father Pie reported high job satisfaction and said he had worked in jail for almost ten years. The Chaplain described his counselling as essential to rehabilitating many prisoners; some had never had a role model to look up to.

Patrick liked the man and believed he served the inmates well. How was he now going to stand by whilst the man was put into hospital or worse so he could take over the post? If only the man had proven to be nasty or abusive of his position or had some dark secret Patrick could exhort. But he appeared a fair, kind, generous tolerant man who had seen and heard a lot while at Wakefield. Patrick could not stand by whilst this poor man was beaten or even killed, but what choice did he have in this dog-eat-dog society?

Patrick thought that perhaps he could find a way to reduce the pain and suffering of Father Pie by offering to poison him just enough to have him off work for a long time but not enough to kill him then that would be preferable to the man being beaten or stabbed or maybe even both.

Patrick went to see Kieran and put his idea to him. Patrick was confident there were enough inmates in this prison to ask advice about the best ways to poison someone allowing for the victim's survival. There must be at least one chemist on the Delaney payroll to concoct the potion.

Surprisingly Kieran agreed without needing persuasion. He said he liked the man too but would never put sentiment before business. But... If Patrick was prepared to administer the poison, and the scheme worked, he would also be happy. He secretly doubted Patrick could do the job, but he would give him a chance.

Kieran consulted with one of the known poisoners on the wing and was advised that Strychnine was available in prison and that mixed with water or food, it is odourless but has a bitter taste, so mixing it with orange juice might disguise the taste. He remarked that only a tiny amount is needed to produce severe effects in people, especially the old or infirm. Kieran just shrugged and said that he was no expert and that if the man died, he died, and it was down to Patrick to decide the dosage. He organised the exchange of Strychnine for tobacco the man could sell on for a profit, and 'Ratty', the poisoner's nickname, arranged that he could deliver within the week.

When the Strychnine arrived, it was concealed as icing that

THE PRICE OF SIMPLICITY

Ratty had coated onto two biscuits. It was arranged that the biscuits would be passed to Patrick with his meal. "For fucks sake, tell him not to be tempted to lick the icing. He will have to wrap them in a hankie and put them in his pocket on the pretence of eating them later."

Patrick was informed of the transaction and the caution needed. He was told after that it was up to him how he gave the Chaplain the Strychnine and how much was required was guesswork. "It's a bit like the three bears story, Patrick, not enough and you fail, and we have to invent an accident to get him into hospital, too much and it's 'Goodbye Pie', just enough and Voila. It will need an extra prayer tonight, Patrick, and that's for sure." Kieran laughed as he relayed the instructions, enjoying the gamble. His firm had thought it was so good they were laying odds on the Chaplain's outcome. Patrick shook his head at the barbarity of the men. Still, he preferred the odds of Father Pie, living from the poison to being savagely beaten.

In the meantime, Patrick was told to step up his Christian endeavours. It would be made known amongst the prison population that the Delaney brothers would only take religious studies from an ordained Catholic priest like Patrick. Others would follow, and by the time you 'DO' the Chaplain, you will have your own congregation. Then, the deal should be done when Chester drops to his knees and forgives his tormentor. Kieran added, "Ok, Patrick, now off you go and be a good boy before you poison the Padre." Kiernan's laughter rang around the walls of his cell. As the others in his firm joined in the joviality, the prisoners in the corridors looked towards the cell to see what was happening.

The first attack in Patrick's presence made him feel sick. He felt so sorry for the man who had put his trust in Patrick, although he was watching the door throughout his forced confession. When the door burst open and the beating began, the man was further ridiculed when one of his attackers said, "The fucking NONCE has pissed his pants, the dirty fucking bastard."

Patrick hadn't been aware that the man was a NONCE; the man had not confessed anything, even bordering on that sort of perversion. Instead, the man had spoken of racketeering and stepping on a few toes. His illegally derived income was for blackmailing vulnerable businessmen with a threat to expose them by capturing footage of them in a compromising or embarrassing situation. This usually involved buying or selling drugs. Unfortunately for this man, one of his victims worked for the Delaney brothers and the firm needed to make an example of the man. As the attackers affirmed, he was lucky to survive such a brutal attack. "You were taking the piss, mate, trying to extort money from one of the Delaney boys. Didn't you think to check out the credentials of your victims?"

In this instance, NONCE was used purely as an insult, not a label. The would-be confessor was taken to the hospital and had been lucky not to lose an eye.

The constant threat of brutality was challenging to get used to. Although there were fights of some nature every day, Patrick was off limits until the prisoners were told otherwise. Patrick knew he had no certainty of safety for his life sentence. He spent nights alone in his cell trying to find ways to bring in contraband or some other form of benefiting the Delaney boys. He was afraid there would come a time when he was no longer helpful and would be thrown to the dogs and everyone inside who had no worth to the powerful gangs.

This first glimpse into gang life horrified Patrick. Still, it was nothing compared to what he was to witness in the coming months, where he was powerless to intervene. He was a silent witness to the mutilation of protruding parts of the body (lips, tongue, hands, genitals, nose, ears), all performed as a judicial punishment amongst the prison population. The Delaney's told

THE PRICE OF SIMPLICITY

him they had to prove now and again that they were more frightening, brutal and more muscular than their counterparts and if Patrick's worse fear was gang rape, to be sure, there were far more heinous punishments to be had if the Delaney's were betrayed.

For more severe punishments, prisoners were harmed through scalding, burning, immersing in boiling water or boiling oil, and even putting inside ovens, many never regaining consciousness. This was the life that Patrick had signed up for and one that he begged forgiveness for each and every night when he was alone in his cell. Patrick's only saving grace was that men who would not usually attend Church had started to visit the cell set aside for Catholic Mass each Sunday and participate in the confessional. He was not there to judge. Patrick reminded Delaney and the men of their firm that a Catholicism confession to a priest is considered a confession to God himself, and the Almighty runs his own criminal justice system.

Father Pie had been to visit Patrick and his newly formed Catholic Church, the transformed cell. He had been impressed with the number of attendees Patrick drew to his Sunday Mass. Father Pie was not a jealous man. Knowing Patrick was an ordained priest who had acted in good faith albeit unguided, he offered to help him set up and share the chapel he used. He offered a compromise whereby they could use the chapel on a Sunday, Father Herron could take the mass, and Father Pie would be on hand to administer any religious guidance to non-Catholics either during or after Patrick's Holy Communion.

Patrick knew sooner or later he would have to remove Father Pie. Still, by working with the Governor's blessing, he would help legitimise his future plans and appease the Delaney's into the bargain. That night Patrick slept peacefully for the first time since arriving in Wakefield Prison, without all the dogs of hell chasing him around his prison cell whilst Patrick slept. Instead, he dreamt of Elizabeth, stroking her hair, looking into her eyes, and feeling her body. This was like a dream come true; Patrick had got his foot in the door of the chapel quicker and more amicably than he ever would have imagined.

When the lights went on, signifying it was time to wake up, he felt a pang of regret that he had not consummated his relationship with Elizabeth that night. He was thirty-five and had never been intimate with a woman. Although he believed in marriage, he could not be held responsible for his night dreams. Now, his illicit longings interrupted his daydreams too. He was a changed man, whereas he had always longed for Elizabeth to be married to her and become the father of her children. He would have left the priesthood and made an honest woman of her. Now, it was as if his faith was convenient as Patrick longed to make love with her night or day, with or without marriage. He could tell her of his deep desires if only she would visit him. Not to frighten her but to let her know that 'HE' was as much a man as anyone she knew, and he would gladly put her before the Church or his chosen profession. Patrick wanted her to see that he had made a mistake that night by not listening to her and shunning her so he could rescue Rosie; he knew that now. Although the rescue had been successful, he now believed the police could have managed it without him. He could be lying in the arms of the woman he loved instead of planning the best way to poison a man he liked and admired through fear and intimidation.

He had never before felt free to fantasise about women. Once he started, he could not stop, and the fantasies excited him and made him long for them to be confirmed. Patrick used to believe that as a priest, he was obliged to love everyone in a platonic way. But not allowed to love anyone or be loved by anyone in the physical sense. Now he believed the love between two consenting adults was a gift from God and should therefore be cherished, not hidden or ignored. He felt like a fool for

THE PRICE OF SIMPLICITY

seeing this wrongly all this time. Patrick knew this was not the teaching of the Catholic Church, but he felt not everything taught by the Church was fully understood. He now believed that we should question the words not of God but of the men that translated God's word because, after all, they were human beings and, as such predisposed to make errors no matter how well-intentioned their words were.

Patrick knew that sometimes, mortal man has to make decisions that may be offensive to some but beneficial for the greater good. His door opened as he lay considering these thoughts, and he was instructed to leave his cell; it would be searched. To Patrick's knowledge, nothing in his cell could incriminate him. Still, another prisoner may have planted something at any time, and he would have to pay the consequences.

Patrick got out of bed and left the cell and had to wait outside whilst the officers tipped up his bed, threw his belongings on the floor and ransacked the compartment. When it was over, the officers left, and he was told to return and tidy up. Chester appeared as he began putting things back; Patrick noticed that he showed no surprise at what had happened. Patrick turned to him and asked. "Why?"

"I notice you have become very comfortable in your new position in the Church alongside the Chaplain. You should realise that you still work for us and to remind you we can and will take you down in an instant if you betray us. Today the guards found nothing but next time, who knows what they will uncover. Just bear that in mind when you are having your tête-à-tête with Father Pie. AND... Patrick.... It is time to share your biscuits with your new friend. Chester left the cell and winked at Patrick.

It took several minutes for Patrick's heartbeat to steady, the raid had been unexpected, but he had known it must have been sanctioned by someone. Now he knew it was Chester Delaney.

93

This bothered him as he had always dealt with Kieran for anything that needed attention.

Chester was the harder of the two, more vicious and lacking empathy. Not that Kieran was a saint, far from it, but he could empathise, unlike his brother Chester. Patrick hadn't forgotten about the arranged poisoning. Still, Patrick had hoped things could be sorted out without the need to administer the Strychnine; now, it was just a matter of when Patrick had to do it. He intended to go and speak to Kieran later that day and ask when he would like the poisoning to occur. It had undoubtedly interrupted his fantasies regarding Elizabeth; unfortunately, the reality was not quite so pleasant.

TIME FOR REFLECTION

Elizabeth was alone with her girls for the first time in what felt like ages. With her mother away, she wanted to make the most of this weekend and forget about Robert and Patrick. She had heard of a picturesque walk by a secret waterfall called Priestly Green Circular and decided to take her daughters there. They dressed warmly and took buses and a taxi to get there.

As they walked along the muddy path, the girls ran ahead, making up stories and laughing. Elizabeth tried her best to jump over puddles with her unsuitable footwear. But her efforts failed, and she landed face down in a pool. The girls stopped when they heard their mother fall on the ground with a thud, and the silence was deafening as they waited for their mother's reaction. Elizabeth felt embarrassed and ridiculous, but then she laughed, bursting the tension that had held the children frozen to the spot. With relief, the girls joined in, splashing in the muddy water together, wiping their faces on their handkerchiefs.

As they walked through the wood, Lizzie spotted an owl high in a tree, and the three stood mesmerised at the vision. "I thought owls were nocturnal?" whispered Maggie.

"Well, this one's like you and won't go to bed," replied Elizabeth.

Elizabeth's soaked clothes made her shiver as they continued the walk, and she urged the girls to hurry to the end. On the bus ride home, people stared. Still, the girls talked about the fun they had experienced that day. Elizabeth realised that no man was worth sacrificing time with her children, and for once, she didn't care what other people thought.

When they were almost home, Elizabeth suggested getting off the bus one stop early to buy fish and chips and eat them as soon as they got home. This was the best news she could have given her children, and as they began to thaw out at home, eating their feast in their pyjamas, they declared that the day had been the best of their lives. This made Elizabeth glow inside, and she thought, at last, she had become a good mum for her children. Tonight she would write to Patrick and tell him she would not be seeing him again.

Her life had changed so much since she first met the alluring, dynamic priest, Father Herron. She had blushed so much the first time she saw him, wondering if he could tell how much she desired him. For the first time, she felt so bewildered by a man she could not speak, her words were getting jumbled, and Elizabeth knew she was making a fool of herself. How good life had been back then, she had a husband, a daughter and her whole life ahead of her, and even though she had started to feel the shortcomings of poverty, she still felt young.

The memory of Patrick was now fading, she had had a brief fling with Robert, and although they didn't have sex, there had been intimate hugs, kisses and fondling that had aroused Elizabeth and awakened desires that she had forgotten. With Patrick, it had all been in her imagination, her wild fantasies, her dreams and illusions just a pipedream. With Robert, it had been real, felt, not just imagined. Elizabeth had experienced mutual, hungry desire. He was attainable if she had given into his cravings instead of insisting on marriage. Or even forgiven him for his foolish behaviour with Beryl, they may still have been together. Yet she couldn't turn the clock back. She once again had to move on.

It was better to move on, especially now that Molly had found the advert for the singles club they would try. Even if she didn't meet the man of her dreams, at least she would be trying to get a life and not sit night after night moping for something that only happened in her head. Yes, she believed her life would improve; she had enjoyed a wonderful day with her children without needing her mother to be there. The best bit was the children enjoyed it too.

Elizabeth settled down on the settee and began her letter to Patrick. As it was the last letter she intended to write, she wanted to be as truthful as possible, explain all her feelings no matter how hard it was and say goodbye to her delusions for good. Yet it wasn't until she was on the fifth edition of the letter that she began writing from her heart and not her head, and once Elizabeth started, she couldn't stop. It was an outpouring of sexual tension, the tears of a broken heart, and feelings of complete and utter helplessness, guilt and anxiety that had plagued her over the years. Her words flooded onto the page like a waterfall of emotion, pounding the rocks below with the hurt she had endured, seeping into every crevice of every meandering turn the cacophony of her silent screams of frustration. Page after page of her innermost sentiments fell and shattered into a thousand words broken, unrepairable, destroyed and defeated.

When she had finished, Elizabeth felt exhausted. She walked wretchedly up the stairs to bed, where she wrestled with her demons throughout the night. She stood at the water's edge in her dream, looking into a deep ocean. Elizabeth had always had a fear of water, and this made the invention even more horrific. As she looked out, she saw the incoming waves getting higher and more forceful Elizabeth began to panic; her feet wouldn't move. She was trapped where she stood. Then Elizabeth felt a tiny hand touch hers and looked down to see a child looking up at her, afraid. Elizabeth knew this was the end, and they were about to die, but she could not look away or move her feet no matter how hard she tried. The child held on tighter to her hand, trusting her to save them. As the incoming wave grew in enormity, she realised this was the one that would kill them. She bent down towards the child and whispered let's turn and look at the hills. They both slowly turned, and Elizabeth held her breath, waiting for the wave to engulf them, her heart beating furiously, the child squeezing her hand, trusting her. Elizabeth took a last gasp of air, holding it until her throat burned and then....

Elizabeth awoke sweating, gasping, panting, and so grateful to lie in bed; she had never had such a vivid dream about dying. What had the vision meant? She prayed it was not a premonition of what was to come. Fleetingly, Elizabeth wondered about her mother with Vera at the seaside and thought maybe something terrible had happened. Like a sixth sense, this dream had alerted her to a death that had occurred or would occur soon? Nothing was clear, apart from the fear she now experienced. Elizabeth got out of bed and looked into the room where her children lay so peacefully, unaware of her night terror. She would post the letter immediately and rid the house of this evil.

NEW EVIDENCE

Patrick's congregation was growing, and he heard the confessions from many prisoners. Patrick's reputation as a fair, non-judgemental priest that knew a bit about the world was spreading. One day when one of the cons, a London gangster named 'Joey the toes' on account he didn't have any, walked into the confessional, Patrick's interest was more than sparked when he mentioned a familiar acquaintance Bill Black. Joey was on the pay role of the infamous Kray Bothers and had been sent north to do business with Bill Black in an introductory capacity. "I wasn't right happy about it as it goes. If you understand my meaning, I don't like dealing with 'Ponce's and Nonces.' Recounted Joey.

At hearing the name Bill Black, Patrick froze. Bill was the only person alive who could verify that Jack had kidnapped the underage girl to sell her to the highest bidder. He could validate Patrick's evidence that he had only been involved in rescuing the girl and freeing her from Jack's clutches. But how was Patrick going to get this man to help him? The Delaney's would only allow him secure evidence for his release once he had proved his worth. Patrick had no power in this place; right now, he was worth more to Delaney's inside than on the outside. The scam they had been preparing for these last few months was almost ready to reap the rewards.

Patrick had listened, with a growing curiosity, to Joey talking about meeting up with a 'foreign geezer', as Joey put it, in Manchester to bring him to Huddersfield to inspect a girl that was going to be taken south. Joey disliked the man, but he had a job to do, so he did what he had been paid for.

But whilst he was in Manchester, he had been instructed to pick up a face that had fled London still owing a substantial amount of money. "Well, to cut a long story short, I chopped his bleeding head off. It wasn't until the next day that I learned that I had done the wrong geezer." Joey laughed aloud.

"Well, I am sorry about that, especially because I now had to return and get the right bloke and do him. I had both heads in my car when the cops pulled me over driving from Huddersfield back to the smoke. They had started to go off by then, too, and my bleeding car stunk worse than the foreigner I was taking back to London with me. Anyway, we both got busted, and that bleeder went down too. He is in here somewhere, I believe."

It was hard to know what part of the story Joey confessed to and which he wanted to atone for. Every time Joey opened his mouth, he spoke of another atrocity. Patrick assumed Joey was sorry for killing the wrong man but wasn't sure. Most inmates who came to confession didn't see their crimes as needing forgiveness; they wanted atonement for its effect on their families. Leaving children and parents who had to live with the shame of what they had done. Struggling to make ends meet or missing significant events in their family's lives. These were the crimes as far as they were concerned and what they longed to be forgiven for. What Patrick really wanted to do was have a chat with this man when he wasn't in the confessional. Patrick needed as much information as possible to present his solicitor with new evidence in the hope of a re-trial. Patrick needed help, and he decided to make a deal with the Delaney's, Kieran, if possible so that they would help him.

He would also need to find a way of befriending Joey to get him to talk about his time in Huddersfield because knowledge is power. Even without the help of Kieran Delaney, the more

THE PRICE OF SIMPLICITY

Patrick could find out, the more chance he would have.

In every anxiety dream Patrick had experienced late, he was helpless to make things right, relying on scum like the gangsters controlling his new world. As he reflected in the sanctuary of his cell, he realised that the pain of the trauma he had experienced had momentarily crippled him. He could not move forward physically or mentally and needed to rest and be emotionally productive. But now, the coiled snake that lay at the base of his spine had awakened to pierce the artery of life within Patrick, making him more assertive and fearsome to his foes. Kieran and Chester would never recognise this awakening that would end the oppression placed upon Patrick.

But in the cold light of day, Patrick began to understand that he was not a helpless man deprived of any movement. He was intelligent and needed more practice playing the game and inventing rules. Dawn was awakening Patrick in every sense. This traumatic experience had placed him on a path of emergence. The catalyst was hearing Bill Black's name again; it was time to shed the skin of doubt and become the ultimate predator. He was getting stronger and stronger with a more fervent following.

Patrick had started life so innocently, looking to his parents for guidance, but soon realised he was at the mercy of his father's moods that overshadowed all his previous emotions. He felt fear. The fear in his life manifested when he realised his well-being meant nothing to his father. He was owned and oppressed.

When Patrick escaped to the Seminary, he relinquished all personal desires to serve God and repent for any sins that had led him on this path. Patrick was drawn to seeking more profound meaning and awakened spiritually, learning to help others, not himself. Patrick devoted himself to God, wishing only to save people from their own destruction.

Patrick's problem was he still had an ego; he had to prove and gain recognition that Patrick was righting wrongs and was the only man for the job. Patrick failed to reach 'Totality'; his ego was still at the centre of his life. Now he had reached a junction in his life, a crossroads.

When he had left for Spain, he had genuinely believed that the material world was a prison, and Patrick had longed to follow the spiritual path leading to the unbounded freedom of the Spanish Mountains; Patrick thought that if he found the right direction, he would undoubtedly find inner peace. Patrick hoped to rid himself of his past life and the shame and suspicion that had pursued him since his father turned him into a monster.

HOME AT LAST

Margaret recognised that the day would be difficult for her sister Vera when she left Scarborough to go home. Owen lit Vera's world and put a spark back into her life that had been missing for a while. Margaret surmised that her problem with Vera moving to Scarborough and leaving her family behind was her own jealousy. Margaret had questioned why she could not find a man she could fall in love with. Where were the admirers that used to hound her? How had her sister, who had never matched up to Margaret in intelligence or looks, been the one to find love? It wasn't fair. Margaret knew she was sometimes hard to get on with and could be domineering. But that was only to safeguard those she loved and protect her feelings.

Later that day, Vera would have to face Owen and tell him it was all over and hopefully give him a piece of her mind for deceiving her for so long. Margaret guessed Vera would move back to Huddersfield, and at least she would have her sister back. The bus ride seemed to go on forever. She had hoped to call in on Elizabeth to see the girls and give them their stick of rock and tell Elizabeth all about Owen being married. At least the show had been good that they had been to see; it was always nice to get out and do something a bit different.

Margaret presumed that Elizabeth had been sitting at home all weekend, and the girls would have been bored to death and dying to see their nanna. She felt important in their lives and wished she had gone on to have more children. If she had, Elizabeth would not have been an only child and more independent; Margaret's life would have been taken up with the fun of chasing children around.... She may still be married to Charles.

Margaret had nodded off on the bus, dreaming about trying to find all her children, which were no more significant than her thumb. Some were falling down drains, others were rolling off tables onto the floor, and they were all so cold. In her dream, she lit the oven to put them in to get them warmed quickly so that they didn't die. But then she had forgotten them as she raced around looking for the ones she had lost. Margaret was in total panic. Nobody was about to help her look, and she was overawed by the pressure of looking after so many tiny children. She was screaming and shouting for help when she was startled awake by another passenger on the bus watching Margaret during her nightmare. She only intervened when she began calling out. "Are you alright, lovey? You were terribly upset earlier. Is someone meeting you off the bus? Perhaps I can call you a taxi?"

Margaret was dreadfully embarrassed she could still remember the dream that had plagued her. She assured the woman she was alright and that she was overtired, which must have resulted in a nightmare. After retrieving her case from the luggage area, Margaret insisted on going home and almost ran to the bus stop. On reflection, Margaret thought she would see the children tomorrow; it was better to get home and have a good night's sleep; things were obviously getting on top of her.

When she got home, the house was freezing; it was mid-November and felt like mid-winter. She was grateful at least a new gas fire had been fitted, and the chimney from the coal fire had now been blocked off. Instant heat is what she needed, and a strong cup of tea. The only problem with having a gas fire was that it didn't send any heat upstairs, and she knew it would be even colder in the bedroom. She hurried up the stairs to put the electric blanket on before coming to watch the news and have

THE PRICE OF SIMPLICITY

supper. Margaret realised she hadn't eaten anything for at least six hours, so she toasted some crumpets Margaret had bought in Scarborough. As the butter slid across the crumpets and dripped into the holes, Margaret sighed in satisfaction. It was good to be home; she only hoped Vera was doing ok.

Margaret woke unrefreshed but needed to get to work; she wanted the day to be over so she could see the girls again after school ended. The girls were delighted with their sticks of rock and wanted to check if the writing that went around the tip and tail of the candy stick went the whole way through. Margaret sent them outside to investigate Maggie had grabbed a knife and the rolling pin to hammer against the blade to slice the candy stick, and already shards of sticky sugar were flying everywhere.

Margaret had worked until 3:00pm to finish in time for the children coming home from school. She was tired after a restless night, an early start and washing to do. Monday was the traditional washing day. Everyone who shared the communal hanging ground had days and times to peg out their washing. It was rare for anyone to put anything out in winter; instead, they had to dry the clothes around the fire indoors. Margaret had a large wooden clothes horse placed in front of the gas fire blocking the heat from the room, but needs must. The children didn't care as long as they could see the television. "Did you go on a donkey nanna?" piped up Lizzie.

"Of course, she didn't; she's a woman and too big. She would break the donkey's back." Laughed Maggie.

"Don't be so cheeky, Maggie, I could go on a donkey if I wanted to, but it was too cold for donkeys this time of year." Explained Margaret as the door opened and Elizabeth entered, relieved that her mum was back and the children were again being cared for after school.

CAUGHT IN THE ACT

Lizzie was finally becoming more independent, making her own friends and relying less on her sister Maggie. While she wasn't quite ready to venture too far from home, she enjoyed playing in the nearby streets. She felt confident in her ability to handle herself.

Meanwhile, Maggie was relishing her newfound freedom. With her own group of friends, all boys, she revelled in the attention they gave her. She quickly learned how to play them, making herself even more desirable. And when one of her closest friends, Craig, became her boyfriend, Maggie felt truly cherished. He fiercely protected her, and she loved feeling superior to other girls.

As Craig and his friends started high school, they began to seem much older than Maggie. They spent their time in the quadrangle of Oakes Junior School, riding their bikes, swearing, and talking about all the exciting things they could do. Craig would ride his bike at breakneck speed with Maggie perched on the handlebars, basking in the jealousy of the other boys. And when they started experimenting with smoking, Maggie eagerly joined in, relishing the feeling of acting so grown up.

But it wasn't just smoking and bike-riding that the high school boys were interested in. They had started climbing onto the school's roof, daring each other to walk around the perimeter. They always watched for the caretaker, who was known to be fierce with trespassers. Despite the risk, the excitement was

THE PRICE OF SIMPLICITY

too much to resist. Each time they would venture higher and further, Maggie would need lifting up at each rise as she was too short to get footing for the climb.

The group had determined that today was the day they would do it! They would climb the highest section of the school and tie a piece of cloth to the steeple to prove to everyone that they had the guts to do it. And anyone who didn't make it would be a chicken.

The tallest and strongest boys led the way while Maggie followed at the back, relying on their help to pull her up each time. They ran on the narrow ledges to avoid being seen, but as they turned the corner, they heard the caretaker's voice warning them to get down or he would call the cops.

But they were so close to their goal that they decided to speed up, despite the slippery tiles from the recent rain making the climb more dangerous. Craig almost slipped and collided with Maggie, who struggled to grasp the wet slate tiles.

Thankfully Craig managed to grab onto a section of the roof and regain his balance. The end was in sight; one final leap across from one building to the other, and they would be there. The last ledge tapered, making it hard to move at speed, but as they reached the edge, one after the other made the jump. Maggie started falling behind, and she could hear the caretaker shouting, "Get down, you stupid kid. You are going to break your neck."

Maggie realised he could not see the others, only her, as she was far behind. In front of her, she could hear Craig shouting for her to hurry up, and she tried to move faster. But when Maggie got to the jump between the buildings, the gaping hole that separated her from the boys seemed too challenging to achieve without a run-up. The ledge was too narrow to turn around, and she started backing up around the corner to gain momentum on her approach. Maggie started to doubt her ability to make the leap. As her heart beat faster, drumming against her chest, her breath was getting harder and harder to escape from her gaping mouth. The shouts in front and, more frighteningly, from behind seemed to echo in her head. Maggie started telling herself, "Do it, come on, just do it."

She started running up when suddenly, from behind her shoulder, she was grabbed. She looked into the red, angry face of the caretaker as he slammed her against the roof. "You stupid little bitch! What the hell are you doing up here?"

He turned her around and pushed her ahead, keeping hold of her jumper. Craig and the others had seen this and hidden, waiting for him to go.

Maggie was more worried now than when she had seen the chasm she was meant to leap over. She had no choice but to return with this big, angry man. What would her mum say? What if he called the police? What if he murdered her up here on the roof? She sniffled and trembled as he forced her to return to the quadrangle where the hole was to get back down. It seemed to take forever with him berating her the whole way.

When they finally reached the hole, the caretaker climbed down and lifted her down too. Maggie could clearly see him shaking with anger, his mouth pinched together, his face red and eyes wide and terrifying.

But Maggie was not one for tears and bravely bit into her lip to stop herself from breaking down. He almost dragged her to his house, where his wife stood on the step with her hands on her hips. She called out that the police were on their way and to keep hold of the kid until they arrived.

At this, Maggie's shoulders slumped; she knew she was in trouble. Maggie was frightened that she would be sent to Borstal,

THE PRICE OF SIMPLICITY

a place her mother often spoke about when Maggie had done something terrible. Her mum had told her that Borstal was for out-of-control children, and it was similar to prison and very harsh indeed.

Maggie had no idea what she would say to the police when they arrived. She knew she wouldn't grass on her friends and wondered if they would torture her in Borstal to get the information out of her. Maggie thought that although she had done plenty of naughty things, this was the first time she had been in trouble with the police. Maggie had seen on the television they sometimes gave you a chance if it was your first offence, and she crossed her fingers to try and get some good luck.

Elizabeth finally felt like life was giving her a chance to rebuild the life that had seemed so doomed until now. She and Molly were about to embark on a grown-up adventure that Elizabeth hoped would conclude in love. At last, Elizabeth had long periods when both the girls were out playing in the area with their friends, which gave her time to read the books Elizabeth devoured each week after visiting the library. She had started a new thriller and emersed herself fully into the author's world when startled by a loud banging at the door.

When Elizabeth rose to answer the door, notions of who it could possibly be danced in and out of her head. It was too loud to be one of the children's friends, so it must be an adult; she wasn't expecting anybody and her curiosity was aroused.

When she opened the door, she was horrified to find a police officer standing on the doorstep with Maggie by his side. Her immediate thoughts were of Lizzie, and fear gripped her as she gasped and asked: "What's wrong?"

The police officer calmly asked her, "Is this your daughter Ma'am?"

Elizabeth nodded slowly and asked, "Has something happened to Lizzie, Maggie?"

"The police officer looked at Elizabeth and said, "I think your daughter has some explaining to do. She has been reported for trespassing and is lucky not to have killed herself today."

Elizabeth looked at Maggie, shaking her head and telling her to get to bed. She then asked the police officer what had happened. She would speak to her later. The officer explained that he had received a call from the caretaker of Oakes Junior School that a child or children were messing about on the roof. The caretaker climbed up, risking his own life to get your daughter; he paused and looked at his notebook, 'Maggie' down, before she fell off and broke her neck.

Once the officer had gone, Elizabeth called Maggie down and asked why she had been so stupid. Maggie couldn't find a good enough reason. Her mum was clearly furious, and Maggie knew the outcome would not be good. After speaking angrily and criticising Maggie for her irrational thoughtlessness, Elizabeth said, "I have lost one child. Do you really think I want to lose another one? Get upstairs and don't come down again the rest of the day; I am so cross with you, Maggie, I could hit you." Maggie disappeared quickly before her mother had a chance to release her anger.

An hour later, there was another loud knock at the door; Elizabeth thought it might be the officer returning to check on Maggie. When she opened the door, there was another police officer, this time with a defiant-looking Lizzie. Elizabeth could not believe her eyes as she stared at Lizzie and then the policeman standing by her side.

Elizabeth's heart dropped as she heard the officer's words. Her little girl, a thief? This couldn't be happening. But there was no denying it; her daughter had been caught red-handed, stuffing her pockets with sweets from the corner shop.

The officer continued, "Your daughter's excuse was that she was 'helping herself' because the owner wasn't there. Can you believe it? The audacity of this kid!"

Elizabeth couldn't help but chuckle nervously at the situation. This was the second time Lizzie had been caught taking things that didn't belong to her, and the second time she didn't appear to have any conscience about it. Elizabeth was at her wit's end, the second visit from the police in one day; what would she do?

Thankfully the owner had agreed not to press charges on the proviso that Elizabeth went into the shop to apologise and pay for the sweets, totalling two shillings. The shame of facing the shopkeeper, who would tell all the neighbourhood about Lizzie. Elizabeth swore she would not dare show her face in the area. She turned to Lizzie, "What do you think your nanna and daddy will say about your stealing Lizzie?"

Lizzie sulkily replied, "I don't know; please don't tell them."

Elizabeth ordered Lizzie upstairs to bed; and shut the door. Elizabeth stood for several moments, trying to make sense of everything before sloping back inside. Elizabeth would have to go to the shop sooner rather than later and sort it out, but she would need to build up some courage first. She wondered if her mother would go with her; she would tell her tomorrow and ask her advice.

GOODBYE FATHER PIE

The biscuits he had hidden in a napkin for the last few weeks were stale. Still, the icing could easily be transferred onto some freshly baked cookies that Kieran had delivered to Patrick before Mass. The order had been given; after a successful Mass on Sunday, Patrick would stay behind, as always, to have a cup of tea with the Chaplain, a routine Patrick had built up to eliminate any suspicion when the time came to bring the laced biscuits along.

Patrick felt nervous, but he had spent time in the library trying to find out as much as he could about the effects of Strychnine on a human. It had been a covert mission trying not to alert the guards that he was looking into poisons, especially when he knew the cause of Father Pie's misfortune would be Strychnine. Patrick would be the prominent first person of interest in the poisoning, which Patrick hoped could be passed off as accidental food poisoning rather than murder.

The Mass that Patrick had prepared was all about 'forgiveness' as shortly after Father Pie's unfortunate demise, there would be an incident where Chester would be insulted and would claim Patrick's sermon on forgiveness had inspired him to forgive the man who he would usually have taken out repercussions on. Everything would fall into place, and the Governor would be persuaded that Patrick should replace Father Pie as the prison priest.

Patrick began his sermon by explaining that he wanted to

THE PRICE OF SIMPLICITY

explore what it means to forgive another person. "We will learn how God forgives us, what Christ teaches about how we should forgive others, and the joy, peace, and love we feel when we forgive. The scripture reading that Patrick chose was 'The Prodigal Son' - Luke 15:11-24.

After the sermon, Patrick spoke to the congregation. "Many of us have done things we're ashamed of. Some are small things, and some might be big or devastating. Forgiveness was so important to Jesus that he forgave the criminal on the cross. He promised the 'good thief' that he would be saved and with Him in paradise."

Patrick continued, "Suppose we reflect on the 'Prodigal Son' where the father humiliates himself to show the son how much he loves and forgives him. I would like all of you to reflect on your life and think about forgiveness."

As arranged, the congregation applauded Patrick, and the Mass ended with congratulations; even the guards were surprised by the turn of events.

Once everyone left to return to their cells, Patrick and Father Pie began to collect the hymn books and tidy up. When the cleaning was complete, Patrick and Father Pie sat down to enjoy tea and the biscuits Patrick had brought him that day. As they reflected on the reaction to the sermon, Father Pie took one of the biscuits and dunked it into his tea. He saw Patrick watching him and apologised for this terrible habit adding 'I always feel biscuits taste much nicer when they are soggy with tea."

Patrick laughed nervously, disheartening Father Pie, "I'm sorry, Patrick. Are you disgusted by my bad habit? I don't have to do it?"

Patrick replied that he was not disgusted in the least he just wasn't feeling well and had a bit of an upset tummy. "Maybe I ate too many of these delicious biscuits earlier?"

Father Pie nodded and took a second one, repeating the process of dunking it into his tea. Patrick looked away, pretending to rub his tummy; his guilt was even worse than he had expected. He needed to get a grip, or Father Pie would begin to be suspicious, so Patrick turned and smiled at Father Pie and started chatting away as if nothing was amiss.

Less than fifteen minutes later, Father Pie doubled over, gripping his stomach, stiffening and gasping for breath. Concerned, Patrick took hold of his shoulders, asking what the trouble was, knowing full well the effects of the poison already taking effect. Patrick needed the poison to work well enough to put Father Pie into the hospital, so he was trying to delay alerting the guards of his obvious distress. Within the next five to ten minutes, Father Pie started having seizures. Still, Patrick knew if he received treatment too quickly, he would undoubtedly recover fully soon. Patrick needed the effect of the poison to have done at least some damage before he was taken to the hospital.

Patrick picked the Chaplain up and carried him to the make-shift stage at the front of the Chapel. He carefully laid the man down and tried to loosen his tie to allow him to breathe a little easier. Father Pie continued to fight for breath, pushing Patrick away and clawing at his neck. Patrick stood back watching, unsure when to call for help, knowing that he was doomed if the Chaplain fully recovered too quickly. It was the Chaplain or Patrick now, and only one would survive if they were both in prison.

Eventually, Patrick could not stand to see the man suffer any longer and called for the guards and had to stand back whilst they assessed the Chaplain's condition. A stretcher was called for, and Father Pie was taken away. Patrick slumped on one of the chairs, agonising over what he had done to an innocent man. What had he become that he could do such a thing to a good man like Father Pie?

Not long after, he was sent back to his cell, where he sat contemplating the metamorphosis that was taking place in his body and mind. Patrick questioned his own sanity. Had he always had this tendency to maim and kill? Was it nature or nurture that had started the change in him? Patrick knew human beings have basic needs, and one of them is to survive by any means necessary, and no one knows their limits until they are put to the test. Should he feel so bad about what he had done? Patrick asked himself if he could have prevented it by choosing an alternative. But then Patrick knew this was the alternative; the Delaney's intended to eliminate the Chaplain without a second thought to satisfy their survival needs. Who was wrong, and who was right?

News spread fast that the Chaplain had been rushed to the hospital following the Mass, and most prisoners assumed he must have had a heart attack. A few prisoners called by to offer condolences or to find out the gossip. It didn't take long for Kieran to send word that his presence was requested, and Patrick slowly made his way to Kieran's cell.

When Patrick went inside, Kieran said he had already spoken to the Governor, expressing his concern that the prisoners needed a Priest to guide them and help them to come to terms with their crimes so that they could repent and atone. Without admittance of their crimes, it was tough for a criminal to rehabilitate in readiness for release back into society. Kieran had explained to the Governor that Patrick was helping with this process, as prisoners trusted him and were finally admitting they had made mistakes that, in some cases, they had a chance to put right. The Governor had agreed that the guards on duty in the Chapel today had reported that Patrick's sermon about 'forgiveness' had touched many prisoners and guards too. This may be the answer. The Governor told Kieran to leave the idea with him, and he would take it to the board of governors for approval.

During breakfast the following day, the sad news was announced that Father Pie had died at some point last night from asphyxiation due to poisoning of some nature yet to be determined.

Chester looked over at Patrick and smiled.

THE PHOENIX CLUB

After the horrendous weekend of police visits, Vera's bad news and her mother's lack of support, Elizabeth was at her wit's end. She had called into the shop cringing with shame to be made to feel like a criminal and the worst mother ever by the shopkeeper. Elizabeth had paid what was owed and was told to keep her and her tearaway kids away from the shop in the future. "Go shoplift off someone else." Where the parting words she used to Elizabeth's retreating back. Thankfully, no one else had been in the shop to overhear this dressing down.

Elizabeth had cried as she walked back down home. She didn't seem to be able to do anything right; Vera had been right. According to them, Saturday had been the best day of the children's lives, and only one day later, they were both in trouble with the police. They were out of control. Maggie, she could understand, but now Lizzie too, and Lizzie just never seemed to have any remorse. Should she take them both to the doctor?

Monday, when Elizabeth woke up, she gave the children their breakfast. She spoke again about keeping out of trouble, or there would be consequences that they all would regret. Elizabeth was not sure what the reprisals would be yet; Elizabeth had just hoped the words would be enough to get the message across to them. At least, Maggie seemed repentant that she had upset her mother, but Lizzie…

To top off the weekend, she had to face Robert, Beryl, and all the other prying eyes and ears of the mending room. She hoped the village gossips had not noted the news of her visitors over the weekend and then today at least would bring some solace.

As Elizabeth walked up the steps reflecting on everything, anger overtook her shame. She stomped up the last flight of stairs, ready for anyone who said a word to her. Elizabeth was tired of feeling that she was not good enough when she worked hard to do her best. She didn't have a husband to support her and thought it was time to tell other people to mind their business. Elizabeth felt ready to face her critics and more than prepared to face Robert and that slut Beryl. Elizabeth hmphed, proud of herself, standing tall and straight, her head held high; Elizabeth marched into the mending room, daring anyone to say a wrong word to her.

But nobody said anything wrong, it was just pleasantries from all she met, even Robert and Beryl looked sorry when she passed them. As the day progressed, the horror and shame Elizabeth had been subjected to this weekend began to fade. She even smiled later when she told Molly about having two police visits in one day. Molly had two boys and reminded Elizabeth to be grateful her children were fit and healthy enough to be a part of childish pranks; no actual harm had been done. "I have had my fair share of complaints about my two Elizabeth, so don't feel bad. Kids are kids, and we are lucky to have them." Molly remarked when Elizabeth finished telling her.

As they worked, the two women began planning their night out to try out the new singles club they had heard about. They didn't know anyone who had been as most of the menders their age were married and had no call for a singles club. Friday night was only a few days away. The women had to sort out babysitters and outfits and ensure they had enough money left for at least one drink and bus fares for Elizabeth at the end of the week. Molly lived in the town centre, so she did not need to catch a bus.

They both decided to wear slacks and a blouse, smart but not too dressy; they would gauge what to wear the following week once they knew what was what. Molly was to meet Elizabeth when she got off the bus, and they would walk down to the Zetland together, stay for at least an hour to give it a chance and then decide if it was for them. The day passed quickly as the talk of going to the Phoenix Club became more of a reality.

After work, Elizabeth almost skipped across the road to her mother's to collect the children. She breezed into the house with a massive smile. Margaret tightened her lips and commented, "I wouldn't be smiling if both my children had been in trouble with the police."

This wiped the smile off Elizabeth's face, and she looked forlornly at her children, who had both lowered their heads. Elizabeth decided this was not the best time to ask her mother to babysit, so instead asked the girls to collect their coats, and they all left for home.

Elizabeth felt drained by the worry and anguish of the weekend and didn't mention it again; she wanted to have a fresh start and needed to be positive instead of emotionally closing in on herself and allowing the negative things to fester and manifest into something more than they were.

The next day Elizabeth told Molly about the frosty reception her mother had given her when she had collected the children. Elizabeth said she didn't think her mother would agree to babysit for her if her mother knew she was going to a 'Singles Bar'. Molly came up with a perfect solution that would suit them both for this first visit to the Phoenix.

Friday night after work Elizabeth rushed home with the girls and told them she was taking them to Molly's house, where they could play with her two boys for an hour whilst she and Molly popped out. Both girls were excited as this sounded like an adventure, and they liked Molly's boys even though they were a few years older than them. Flo, one of Molly's neighbours, would watch them all for an hour. The women thought that was all they needed to assess the new club, and if they liked it, they could make more permanent arrangements in future.

As Molly and Elizabeth set off into town, Flo fell asleep on the settee, and the four children went out to play hide and seek in the dark around the streets of their home. Maggie and Elizabeth had never played out in the night before but thought it was great fun. They played at knocking on doors and then running away, hoping to be chased by the owners. This only happened at one house, but it was enough to encourage them to return three more times until the owner threatened to call the police, which stopped Maggie in her tracks. Thankfully they returned just in time to see their mothers walking up the road, linking arms and laughing. The children ran inside and sat down, watching the television just as the door opened.

Elizabeth and Molly thanked Flo as she opened her eyes and yawned, telling both women that the children had been well-behaved and had never moved from watching the television all night. The four children looked at each other and smiled knowingly, pleased with the fun they had had. Elizabeth took the girls straight home in an excellent mood. She never stopped smiling all the way home and allowed them to stay up even later to watch a funny, rude program called 'Up Pompeii'.

PATRICK FINDS AN ALLY

Patrick found his guardian angel in an improbable alliance. A hardened criminal with no allegiance to the top cons inside the prison. Like Patrick, he was a man who had a conscience, a man who believed stoically in God and the Catholic faith and would do anything for Father Herron. This man thought Patrick had stood by him when he had nothing and no one without harsh words or judgement. Patrick had listened to the man's confession and helped him come to terms with what he had done before he was sentenced. In return, he was turning into a watchdog and defender. The partnership was perfect, low profile, no threat to the Delaney's, a match made in heaven.

The man, Dougie Farrow, was eighteen and doing life for murdering his stepfather, who had repeatedly raped and beaten his sisters, mother and him over the last eight years. He had lived on the streets until he was finally captured and arrested for stealing food from a deli. He had received very little education over the past eight years as he was kept home most days to conceal his bruises. Dougie was scared from head to toe with a cigarette, hot iron burns, a broken nose, deformed lips due to regular beatings, and a permanent limp.

When Dougie first met Patrick, he was an unknown. The two bonded and became inseparable. Still, Patrick instantly saw in Dougie the pain and hatred he also felt from men that preyed on vulnerable boys to the point of torturous handling Dougie had been subjected to from being a young boy.

Dougie had told Patrick that he had smashed the whiskey glass his stepfather had been holding while he fondled his sister and kicked his mother, who was lying on the floor. Dougie walked in on the scene and said it only took two strides to reach the man before he could swipe the glass from his hands. His stepfather had let go of the girl to slate Dougie to remind him he was a useless imbecile that should have died at birth. But Dougie did not listen. He took a shard of glass and pushed it into his stepfather's throat. Once the blood began to spurt, Dougie couldn't stop. He used the same fragment to gouge out his eyes and remove most of his nose. Then stab him repeatedly in the face. Dougie had continued long after his stepfather died and only stopped when his hands became too slippery with blood to do more damage.

Patrick listened and re-lived this murder in his mind, thrusting the glass with Dougie, knowing the pain would finally stop. When Dougie finished his story and looked at Patrick, he held his hands to Dougie, and they hugged like brothers. Each recognised the other's pain and united in the grief they had lived with for years, understanding what it meant to be free at last of the torment.

The Delaney's tried to break the relationship. Still, Patrick was adamant that Dougie needed the guidance of a trusting man of God that he had not had whilst growing up. Patrick said he felt obliged to protect and tutor the boy. In the end, whilst the Delaney's couldn't see the harm, Patrick could see the advantages of having a robust and devoted prodigy. The Delaney's assumed there was love or sexual interest, but they couldn't have been more wrong; neither of these men would ever choose to have a sexual relationship with another man. This relationship was more potent and more sincere; this was

THE PRICE OF SIMPLICITY

more of a father/son relationship where either man would fiercely defend the other. The bond became fixed, and an unbreakable link of two is far more potent than a man that stands alone, however strong that solitary link is.

After Father Pie's passing and Patrick's re-instalment into the role of prison priest, the demands on him from the Delaney's were almost instant. He was told what to order and from whom, knowing each consignment would be filled with contraband. Patrick would carry the can if the smuggled goods were found, and no association could be proved to link the Delaney's. Patrick was being set up to be a scapegoat for the Delaney boys. Patrick did not have a choice in what was happening and obeyed without question.

Patrick had made a friend out of Joey, the London gangster who knew about Bill Black. He was building trust with him and sharing anecdotes about Jack Harrison, whom Joey had also met before he asked him for help. Patrick hoped that Joey would be the key to his release. After getting the letter from Elizabeth that morning, he was more determined than ever to get out of Wakefield and be with Elizabeth before she met and married someone else.

The letter had come as a shock for Patrick and almost broken him. He was unsure if Elizabeth would use the visiting order he had sent; he hoped she would find a way to visit him no matter how hard, but this letter was final. Patrick read the letter repeatedly and was starting to understand how much he had hurt Elizabeth when he had turned his back on her and gone to Spain without contact in all the years he was there. It wasn't as if she had not been in his thoughts because she had. Patrick's thoughts of Elizabeth had plagued him for years, but Elizabeth didn't know that because he never told her. Even then, after all that time, he had just shown up and expected her to drop everything and be with him, which she would have

123

done gladly, according to the letter. Patrick remembered that night when she had tried to wrestle with him to make him kiss her, make love to her, and stay with her. But... he had simply turned and walked away like he had always done, thinking he was above reproach and that she should remain faithful to him no matter how distant or untouchable he was. How naive he had been and how bloody stupid! Patrick put his head into his hands and thought about all the chances he had been given and thrown away. Reading the letter repeatedly allowed him to have a deeper understanding of the underlying meaning behind the words that Elizabeth had written. She could not love a ghost any longer. If he wanted Elizabeth, he would need to be by her side in the flesh as a physical being, not just a fantasy.

Dougie came by and saw Patrick was distraught over something but kept his distance showing Patrick the respect he thought he deserved. When Patrick looked up, they glanced at each other, and Dougie approached. Patrick indicated a seat for Dougie to sit in. Patrick explained a little about why he was feeling the way he was. Dougie tried hard to empathise but was too young and inexperienced to be a man of the world and needed help understanding the problem. But, he could see that Patrick was upset and knew his presence and friendship would at least afford a little comfort to the man. They left the cell and walked to the 'rec room', where Joey usually hung out. Patrick needed to press Joey for more information before he contacted his solicitor to arrange a meeting.

When Patrick and Dougie returned to the cell, Patrick was happy. Joey had talked openly for the first time in his dealings with Jack and his father, Big John. He said that Jack had always been a good, straight, decent guy, and he had come to like him over the years. Jack had called a 'spade-a-spade', and Joey said he admired that in a man, "It was the drugs that ruined Jack, just like most idiots that fall into the trap; once he was hooked, he wasn't himself anymore."

THE PRICE OF SIMPLICITY

Joey continued, "I knew his father, John, before I knew him. He was a hard man with no fear, was as strong as a bull, and built like one too. I had odd dealings with him when I was younger, and later Jack came on the scene, taking over his father's role. Jack mainly stayed in the north, and I stayed in the south. Then Bill Black got involved in the prostitution racket. Bill knew he could make big bucks supplying young girls to foreigners. Bill contacted Reggie, an old friend from London, and they talked about the supply and demand. Bill had money to throw at the venture, and Reggie put him in touch with the Turks. Bill was using Jack to test the water-selling girls and knew Jack was desperate enough for money to do this job and keep him out of it. I reckon he meant to get rid of Jack after the sale went through anyway, so you did Bill a favour, just a little prematurely."

Patrick hinted at Joey giving evidence on his behalf, and although he didn't say 'yes', he didn't say 'no' either. That was enough for Patrick for the time being, the seed had been planted, and he would make sure it grew favourably over the coming weeks. Patrick's mood had risen after his earlier melancholy. He finally believed he was in with a chance to be freed.

After dinner that evening, Chester sent for Patrick. Patrick went along, knowing they would be upping the ante on some venture detrimental to his release if he was caught, but what could he do? Patrick went to the cell, and Dougie followed at a distance like a devoted puppy. Patrick and Dougie disliked Chester; he was nasty towards those he considered beneath him and enjoyed it when others showed him fear.

Chester asked Patrick about the friendship developing with Joey and why Patrick spent so much time with him. Patrick didn't elaborate. He just said they had become acquaintances as they had people in common. Chester said, "Your relationship with Joey could be useful because he won't suspect a thing when you kill him for me."

Patrick was aghast, he needed Joey, and he needed him alive; if Chester was planning to kill him, it would ruin everything. Patrick instinctively put his thumb against his lip. Deep in thought, he curled his forefinger over his mouth and enclosed it with his other hand, looking at Chester before speaking. "I can't do it; I won't do it. He's my friend. It was bad enough accidentally killing Father Pie; I could see the benefit to you getting rid of the Chaplain. But I have done enough; I take great risks whenever you put a new order through my Church, but I do it anyway."

Chester was furious at Patrick's refusal "YOUR FUCKING CHURCH! DON'T YOU DARE ASSUME THAT YOU CAN MAKE DECISIONS? IF... I TELL YOU TO FUCKING JUMP; YOU WILL JUMP AS HIGH AS YOU CAN. DO I MAKE MYSELF CLEAR?"

The shouting had alerted Dougie, and he stood at the door looking in, checking on Patrick's safety. "Get out and take your 'FUCKING IDIOT' with you." Screamed Chester.

Patrick quickly rose and left, and as instructed, Dougie was alongside him instantly. They returned to Patrick's cell, where he could think; Dougie went with him because he would not leave Patrick's side knowing he had been threatened. When they returned, Patrick briefly explained what was happening and the implications. He told Dougie he needed time alone to decide what to do next. Dougie left, but now he had his own agenda; he knew what was needed and would do it as soon as he got the chance.

A VISIT FROM VERA

On Friday evening, the tension in the air was thick as the children left with Elizabeth, their disagreement over her lack of authority lingering. Margaret was puzzled by the late knock on the door and approached it nervously, shouting, "Who is it?"

"It's me, Margaret; it's Vera," came the reply.
When Margaret opened the door, Vera burst into tears, eyes all puffy, mouth drawn down and looking beseechingly towards her sister Margaret. "What on earth has happened, Vera? Has Owen done something to you?"

But Vera couldn't answer her, sobs hindered any attempt at coherent speech, and she nodded and stepped inside. After a cup of strong tea, Vera began to explain. "After you left, I expected Owen to call round that evening, but there was no sign of him for three days."

Vera wiped her nose and continued. "He came in and stood by the door, I asked him to sit down, and he shook his head. Without any discussion, he just said, 'It's over'. I tried to beg him not to end it, but he wouldn't listen."

Margaret interrupted. "Oh, Vera, you knew he was married; you shouldn't have begged him. You should have rebuked him. He is a liar and a cheat."

Vera answered truthfully saying. "But I loved him, Margaret, and I didn't want to be alone anymore. Having Owen in my life has made me happier than ever. Just to have someone to hold me and someone to have a laugh with. It meant so much to me. Ultimately, I didn't care if he was married as long as I could keep the bit of him that I had loved this past year. Now it's all over."

Vera sobbed again before adding, "But that is not the worst. I was just processing Owen telling me it was over. The next day there was a knock on the door, and when I answered it hoping it would be Owen, a woman I had never seen before, standing on the doorstep, staring at me. We looked at each other and, in the end, I had to ask her what she wanted. She raised her head to look me straight in the eye and spoke."

"I'm Lucy, Owen's wife, and I want my husband back."

Vera paused to wipe her eyes and blow her nose loudly. "I was so shocked I didn't know what to say, but then Lucy continued."

"This house belongs to us, and we want you out by next weekend. I have contacted my solicitor, who says I am within my rights to evict you as you have been committing adultery with 'MY' husband as long as I give you a week's notice. Well, this is your week's notice."

Margaret looked at Vera and said, "It's your fault, Vera, for messing with a married man. You had an idea he was married but chose to ignore it; there is nobody to blame but you and that cheating man you got involved with. It's his wife I feel sorry for."

Vera was angry with herself for being fooled in her fifties and being so upset. She turned to Margaret and said, "I know how stupid and selfish I have been, but I feel so hurt I wish I could get revenge on the man. If I had a chance, I would love to put 'Fiery Jack' in his undies to add some heat to his love life." At that, Margaret and Vera laughed, easing the tension a little.

Margaret put the kettle on and turned the fire up to comfort

THE PRICE OF SIMPLICITY

Vera, who looked like she had been through the wringer. At first, Margaret offered no sympathy as they sipped their tea, and Vera talked about leaving her home for the last time. All the memories seem locked up in that house. I can't even describe how it made me feel walking down the path with my suitcase in hand. I had to put all my furniture into storage, and I sobbed the whole time the removal men were taking the things out. They must have thought that I was barmy."

It was evident that Vera needed to talk some more, so Margaret suggested they have a glass of Sherry before bed to help them sleep. The alcohol eased their mood, and both women sat and cried together as they began to recall the past. Margaret started, "Do you remember the time in our teens when we had a double date with the two brothers who were farmers?"

Vera laughed and said, "Yes, I do remember. It was a disaster! You ended up with the one who couldn't stop talking about his stamp collection, and I got stuck with the one who kept belching loudly."

Vera chuckled through tears, "Oh, I remember we went to a dance where the music was terrible, and the boy's danced like clod-hoppers, standing on our toes and banging into us. Typical farmers."

They continued to reminisce, laughing and crying until early morning. But as they finally went to bed, Vera couldn't help but think about Owen and Lucy. She felt a deep sense of shame and regret for what she had done and knew that she had to face the consequences of her actions. The following week was going to be tough to get through; she only hoped Margaret would let her stay until she got back on her feet.

SISTERS OF MERCY

As a result of Vera's entanglement with Owen, Vera and Margaret found themselves bound together once again by circumstances beyond their control. Vera moved into Margaret's little bedroom and moped around, feeling sorry for herself. Margaret was coming home from work ready to look after the children. Vera would still be lying on the settee reading a magazine, having done nothing all day.

Her homecoming was far from idyllic, and the rows and resentment soon started. Margaret's dominant personality often clashed with Vera's commanding nature, usually over the children. Despite being blood relatives, their shared history did little to foster harmony between them and sometimes added to the hostility. One or the other would bring up past events when they had been proved right, which all added to the growing pressure in the tiny house.

Vera's desperation for independence and Margaret's desire to maintain control created an atmosphere of constant friction within their shared space. Arguments fuelled by their frustrations and the weight of their circumstances became frequent. As the days turned into weeks, tensions simmered beneath the surface, threatening to erupt into a full-blown feud.

After one tremendous argument where the mudslinging was worse than usual, and the oppressive atmosphere became unbearable, Vera stormed out of the house, driven by a burning determination to solve her homelessness. Always the survivor,

THE PRICE OF SIMPLICITY

Vera made her way to the local council, her heart heavy with the weight of her predicament, and in tears, she pleaded for assistance and a place to call her own.

Eyes red and puffy, Vera painted a vivid picture of her dire situation, highlighting her vulnerability and the urgent need for accommodation. The council, empathetic to her plight and desperate to be rid of this wailing old woman, listened with trepidation, recognising the gravity of her and her sister's circumstances.

As Vera poured her heart out, Margaret's dominance and bitterness faded into the background. Vera began telling them of her heartbreak over Owen, explaining that she felt like killing herself and didn't want that on anyone's conscience. Vera showed them her arthritic fingers and told them of her urgent medical needs. When she began talking to the male counsellor about her menopause, he had heard enough. He suddenly recognised her vulnerability and the need for immediate assistance. He assured Vera they would do everything possible to find her suitable accommodation. Vera finally left the council offices feeling a glimmer of hope. She returned to Wellington Street and Margaret to face the music.

When she walked into Margaret's house, she looked around, realising her sister was always there for her, even when she acted like a fool. Vera knew she was hard to live with, too, and prepared to apologise for her behaviour. Margaret had calmed down when Vera stormed out and understood that losing Owen had been hard on her sister, and she could have been more sympathetic. The sisters looked at each other, recognising their loyal bond and love for each other despite their differences. Vera told Margaret of her efforts to find a place where she could send for her furniture, and they could both have their own space again.

She explained that she had been to the council and was hopeful that her imposition on Margaret would soon be over as she had all but been promised a place soon. Even though the idea of Vera moving out soon pleased Margaret, she knew she would miss her as soon as Vera left. Still, at least she would be in Huddersfield and not so far away in Scarborough this time.

At the end of the following week, a letter appeared in the letter box offering Vera a modest but comfortable dwelling, a place she could now call her own, in a village she had never been to before called Meltham. Vera was told she could call for the keys the following Friday and move in any time after. It was an exciting time and a new beginning.

The sisters finally understood that one day they would not have the chance to lean on each other; life was too short for quarrels that broke a family apart. Living together had not been ideal, but they had made it through supporting each other, and looking back realised they had laughed more than quarrelled.

Margaret offered to help Vera move into her new home, and Vera promised not to meet up with any more married men.

EVERYTHING COMES AT A COST

Patrick was in a blind panic over the threat against Joey; he needed to do everything he could to keep him alive. Knowing he had a price on his head made Patrick extremely anxious. He needed to make an urgent request to see his solicitor, find out why Chester wanted Joey dead, and try not to tread on any toes himself.

As soon as he had the chance to request a solicitor's visit, it was done; his next mission was to find Kieran Delaney and speak to him privately about Chester and Joey. He got the chance after morning prayers when he asked Kieran if he could have a word with him alone. Patrick didn't have time to beat about the bush and came out with it, asking Kieran what Joey had done that he needed to be taken out. Kieran smiled and said Chester had told him about your refusal to kill Joey and that he was not pleased.

Kieran began to explain what Joey had done and said you haven't really got a choice, mate; as far as Chester is concerned, it is now you or Joey; you have both pissed him off. Kieran continued, "Chester is annoyed with Joey about some smart comment Joey made to Chester while they were in the yard. Chester was furious and felt Joey had tried to make a fool of him in front of some London associates. Chester can't be seen as the one taking revenge, and with you being his new best friend, we think you should do it. A sort of a double insult, being killed by his friend. If you don't do it, Chester will probably have you both killed."

Patrick had thought long and hard into the night about his dilemma of killing his friend and the man who could seal his release. Finally, in the early hours, he had devised a plan that he now needed to implement. Patrick told Kieran that although he had initially said 'No' to killing Joey, it had been the shock of the request rather than a refusal. After considering Chester's request, he surmised he could use the same method to dispatch Joey as he had used on Father Pie. At this, Kieran clapped his hands and gave a hearty laugh. "Perfect, mate, wait until I tell Chester; he will be tickled pink."

Patrick said he would need more Strychnine and would wait to hear from him when he obtained the substance.

When Kieran left, Patrick slumped in a chair; this time, he MUST ensure he got the dosage right. Patrick had a chance if Joey could survive in the hospital. Kieran and Chester would think he had done his part like he had done to Father Pie, and it would not be Patrick's fault that Joey survived. But, Patrick would need to ensure Joey was in the hospital long enough to speak with Patrick's solicitor and then live long enough to stand up in court and give evidence on Patrick's behalf.

The wait for the Strychnine would give Patrick some time to get to see his solicitor and update him on the new evidence that had come to light. In the meantime, he would have to try and keep everyone calm and bide his time. Patrick continued his friendship with Joey and found snippets of information that may help his case each time they met. Patrick had built trust with Joey and, over time, told him all about finding the papers by accident, Jack's relationship with Elizabeth, a woman Patrick hoped to be with once he was released and his involvement in the freeing of the minor and subsequent false arrest and imprisonment for her capture. Patrick was tempted to tell Joey about the poisoning, but who in the right mind would go along with being poisoned with Strychnine? So decided against it.

THE PRICE OF SIMPLICITY

Within the week, Patrick had verification of the solicitor visit he had requested.

After he spoke to the solicitor and revealed all that had come to light, the solicitor hoped they could have enough evidence to secure a new trial. Patrick had passed names on to the solicitor to contact who may be willing to confirm specific facts without involving themselves fully. The police would have to re-open an investigation, but the wheels of justice were now at least in process. The bad news was it would take months before a re-trial could be affirmed. Even when Patrick pleaded that the principal witness for the defence may be dead by then, it could not alter the slow pace of the law. As the solicitor pointed out, "The wheels of justice turn slowly but grind exceedingly fine,' meaning that the justice system may take a long time to reach a result. Still, they eventually will achieve the correct result if you have patience."

Patrick was pleased with the outcome of his meeting and felt at least somewhat allayed for a positive result. Even without Joey, the police would have new evidence to investigate and grow a case against Jack and Bill Black. Patrick imagined that Cindy and Pearl would be subpoenaed to appear in court, as would anyone else that worked at the club during Rosie's imprisonment.

Patrick continued ordering the hymn books filled with drugs and all the other contraband he was organising to come through the prison gates. Patrick knew the Delaney's were building up enough evidence against him to ensure Patrick never turned on them. He couldn't see any other way of keeping safe besides doing as they asked of him until his release.

It surprised Patrick when one day, Dougie casually asked Patrick if he enjoyed working for the Delaney's. Patrick knew Dougie hated them passionately, especially Chester, a bully. Patrick tried to explain to Dougie that he had no choice and hoped God would

135

forgive him as he had little choice. Dougie asked Patrick what he would do if Delaney died. Would he have to do the same work for someone else? Patrick had never thought about it but guessed that if the Delaney's were dead, the scam would end with them. "Why did you ask that question, Dougie?"

"I was just thinking about what would make you happy and keep you safe. I know you want to be with the woman you love, and I want to help you as much as I can. If, by some miracle, the Delaney's died, I would protect you until you were released. You wouldn't need to work for any more faces." Dougie stopped talking and looked at Patrick like this was a viable option.

"Oh, Dougie, if only life was so simple. People don't JUST die; they live long lives or get killed in a place like this. I am happy having a great guy like you being my friend, and I know you will protect me whenever you can, and I will do the same for you. You and I are two lost souls in a cruel world."

Patrick smiled at Dougie, patted him on the back, and set off to the rec room for a snooker game. As they relaxed and socialised, thoughts never far from either man's head were the Delaney's. They held people's lives in their hands, in fists that suffocated and crushed the life out of their subservient slaves. Chester's mania, narcissistic traits, and inflated self-perceptions of power were fed in prison. It was his kingdom, and he ruled with relish. But no matter how big or powerful you are, everyone has an 'Achilles Heel'; it was time to find Chester Delaney's weakness.

EVERYONE HAS
A WEAKNESS

People assumed because Dougie had received little education, he was dumb and unable to process basic information. But Dougie was a survivor, a boy who had survived against all the odds into adulthood.

Dougie appeared invisible to most of the inmates. His deformed features and speech disorder due to his misshapen lips and mouth made it difficult to communicate with others socially, and people wrongly anticipated that Dougie did not hear or understand what was being said. But, they greatly underestimated Dougie, who was astute in many things that they were not. He could not read books but could read people; he was the bravest of allies but the most fearsome of enemies. He had lived a life of depravity and abuse, learning how to become invisible; from being an infant, he learnt to be silent to avoid beatings. He was a master of survival.

Dougie listened carefully when Chester showed abhorrence at a mouse that ran by, visibly disturbed to the point of panic and anxiety. When it crossed Chester's path, he began beating it so hard that its blood and bones splattered across the rec room. Some drops of its blood landed on Chester, and Chester freaked out, afraid of the remains smeared on his clothing. When Kieran suggested it would have been a lot worse had it been a rat, Chester visibly shuddered and drew his stomach in with his mouth open. His shoulders were forced forward as if he was about to vomit. Dougie stood quietly to one side, an idea developing in his mind. Blind fear and blind panic demonstrate extreme weaknesses that could be used to his advantage. When Kieran added, "With Chester's heart condition, I expect him to croak every time he sees a mouse. A rat would definitely flip his ticker off."

Dougie did not discuss his plans with Patrick; he did not need Patrick's permission, approval or assistance. This was a job Dougie could do on his own; if it failed, then he would die; if he succeeded, then things would begin to change. Because the strong Delaney bond would be shattered, leaving only one link that would not be strong enough to maintain the status developed when the Delaney's were joined.

Dougie had a perfect hiding place for what he needed, and this is where his trust in Patrick was most helpful. Dougie's job was to set out the hymn books before each service and collect them at the end. Nobody gave a second thought to the almost mute Dougie, Patrick's ward when he went about his business in the Church. Nobody knew what Dougie was keeping beneath the stage, out of sight and drugged most of the day to ensure their silence.

Dougie found the rat nest one day when he had gone into the Church to lay out the hymn books. He had entered with the lights off as he liked the dark solitude and felt safe when unseen, a practice he had formed from being a small child. Then, he heard the familiar elaborate high-pitched squeaks, chirps and hissing. Most people would be appalled by the sound but not Dougie.

When Dougie investigated the reason for the noise, it became clear. Most rat noises are undetectable, so Dougie knew the rat felt threatened. If Dougie could gain the trust of this rat, it might prove helpful to him. The rat nest he could see had at least five baby rats, ironically called kittens, so the adult rat sent out a warning. The kittens usually took about three weeks to leave the nest, so Dougie knew he had some time to work with the rat before it disappeared.

As a child, Dougie had spent endless hours locked in cupboards, cellars, and attics. Dougie, for all intent and purposes, studied these verminous creatures. He quickly learnt when they would likely attack, trust, and socialise with a human. After his initial fear of the scurrying animals, they finally became the only living beings he could relate to and make a relationship with.

Dougie began visiting the rat each day, bringing it food, and it wasn't long before the rat became used to these visits and allowed him to approach to lay the food down. Dougie estimated that the kittens were only about one week old when he had discovered them, so this gave him just two weeks before he would drug the adult rat, and the babies would be old enough to leave the nest. Dougie had thought about smuggling all eight babies into Chester's cell when he was in the rec room, but there would be no way of keeping them there and releasing them in the darkness when the door was locked. So, it had to be the adult rat.

Dougie had started building what would become Chester's death chamber, a simple structure that needed very little work. It was just blocking pathways and putting a piece of board across to trap Chester's head when he was enticed to peer into the hole. Dougie knew if he slammed the wooden panel across hard enough to hold Chester, he would undoubtedly have marks to show this, along with bites from the rat that Dougie hoped would be fatal. If Chester lived, Dougie would die. But if Chester died beneath the stage sometime after prayers on Friday morning, it might be hours before he was found, and there would be no proof that it had been the dim wit Dougie who had taken his life. In addition, the longer he was trapped, the more chewing the rat would do to escape. Dougie would have already sealed the hole in the wall where the rat had first appeared, so its only other exit would be through Chester's face.

Once it was done and Chester was dead, Dougie would leave the Church and ensure many people saw him about the corridors to vouch for his whereabouts.

Dougie began to study Chester; he had found his weakness and needed to learn more. Knowing Chester's anger triggers and what might defuse a situation if the plan was not working would be helpful. Dougie would need a safety plan if things began to go wrong, and it would be astute of Dougie to know if he could neutralise Chester's anger or stimulate it to a higher level. Dougie noted that Kieran could usually talk Chester down and rein him in. Sometimes, he let him vent his anger until he was too exhausted to continue. After such episodes, Kieran and Chester would disappear to Kieran's cell, and no one else was permitted to disturb them. Dougie discovered this the hard way.

After one fierce encounter with a rival gang member, Chester had gone berserk, beating the man so severely he had to be dragged off him covered in blood and teeth. Even after the man was unconscious, Chester continued to smash tables and anything else he could get his hands on. Everyone stayed well out of his way, including Kieran, and when it was all over, and Chester was spent, Kieran led him back to his cell and closed the door.

Earlier that day, Patrick had mentioned that he wanted to arrange a meeting with Kieran. Dougie took it upon himself to act as a go-between taking a note that Patrick had written asking for the meeting. Dougie knew if Kieran's door was closed, it was as good as a 'Do Not Disturb' sign. But this was an opportunity to see what happened to Chester after a violent episode, even if it cost him a beating.

THE PRICE OF SIMPLICITY

Dougie approached the door with the note in his hands; nobody realised what he was about to do as he walked down the corridor until it was too late. Dougie knocked on the door; almost immediately, Kieran flung the door open, fists raised, ready to pummel whoever had been stupid enough to disturb him. On seeing it was the half-wit, Dougie, he leant towards him and said, "Fuck off, you idiot." Dougie didn't need telling twice, and besides, he had seen all he needed to see. Chester was fast asleep on Kieran's bed, wiped out by his frenzied episode. It was evident to Dougie that Chester was spent after one of his flare-ups and, like a child, needed to sleep to restore his strength. This was also a weakness as far as Dougie was concerned; if he couldn't get Chester by one means, there were now options that he could consider.

Dougie was rising up the prison ladder of recognition and power without realising it. Dougie's strength was his perceived perception by others that he was weak, an easy target and vulnerable. Dougie would have been a powerful adversary if Dougie had received even an average education and minimal care. But, Dougie's carers had failed him in every way; he had no regular education, less than minimal care and had his brain bashed so many times from being an infant that his thoughts were a little muddled or extreme in their possessing abilities. Yet, his loyalty towards those who positively acknowledged him knew no bounds.

From his first time meeting Patrick, Dougie had formed a devotion and allegiance of trust. Patrick's initial non-judgemental attitude towards Dougie and his confidence in him as a fellow human being saddened and then elated Dougie. He was like a child who had been offered a replacement present beyond his imagination or expectation. Dougie had never before in his life been treated like an equal. He had always been considered sub-normal, unable to function adequately to meet the expectations of 'normal' society. And, to suddenly be seen as a person of some worth was so thrilling in its significance that he would do anything in his power to protect the man that presented him in this light. Dougie believed if he died protecting Patrick, he would have been killed for a good cause.

Dougie had taken the rat a morsel of food each day, so it remained used to being fed at that time, but not enough to abate its hunger. When Dougie arrived with the morsel that day, it contained a sedative that would make the rat sleep until the next day. By the time the sedative wore off, it would be cornered by Chester's giant face.

Dougie knew this was his chance. Chester was on his own; he told him Patrick had good news for him and was waiting in the Church to speak to him privately. As Chester entered the Church and looked around for Patrick, Dougie began to annoy Chester making noises Dougie needed to incite him enough to chase him into the gap underneath the stage at the front of the Church. If he could get Chester to put his head into the opening, then the sliding door that Dougie had made could be pushed across, trapping Chester's head in the hole. Chester would not have room for his arms to force the piece of wood that held his head in the space. Chester would be trapped. Dougie had ensured he could hold onto the sliding wooden door and release the rat inside the small area once he was under the stage. The rat was hungry; it would be afraid of the obstacle that blocked its only escape, and if Dougie's plan worked, it would fly at Chester's face. Dougie had purposely starved the rat for the last three days and knew it would undoubtedly attack anyone that cornered it.

Dougie began to goad Chester, calling him names that insulted him. Chester could not believe the audacity of this simpleton who dared to demean him so freely. He thought Dougie must be high on drugs or insane; no one in their right mind would incite Chester. "How dare you talk to me like that, you 'FUCKING

SIMPLETON'? I will beat whatever you have between your ears, and your 'FUCKING PRIEST' can give you the last rites when you are laid dying or dead.

Chester charged forward, and Dougie quickly rolled into his prepared space under the stage. There was no stopping Chester. He was so infuriated he was determined to teach this imbecile a lesson. Chester dropped to his knees, forcing his head and shoulders under the stage to grab Dougie and drag him out. But, within a second, he felt something slam into the side of his neck like an iron clamp. Chester bucked and writhed but could not get his head free. He realised he was ensnared and began to panic. Chester could not bring his arms and hands into the space, and as he lay on his stomach, Chester realised he could not see a thing. There was no light in the opening he had foolishly pushed his head into, but he could hear something in the hole with him. Chester began to shout to Dougie to free him, using threats that echoed around his head. Then he started trying to bribe Dougie and finally pleading with him, just as he felt the teeth of what he realised was a rat.

Dougie's fear of this confined box that held him tight and the rat gnawing at his nose began to trigger a heart attack. Adrenaline was pumping fiercely through Chester's body; his breathing was coming in gasps, and his ears seemed to rush with liquid. His natural fight-or-flight response to this traumatic event increased his adrenaline to toxic levels preventing blood from pumping around his body. Within ten minutes, Chester lay dead.

Dougie exited the Church, leaving Chester dead below the stage. When Dougie entered the rec room, he made a beeline for Patrick to say "Hi" and then made his way towards the toilets bumping into people on the way.

Patrick saw him and felt sorry for him for the endless teasing and bad-mouthing of the others when they were bored. Today, Dougie wanted that to ensure they would all affirm he was there.

SHELAGH TAYLOR

Most of the time, the beauty of being invisible was that the other cons would not have noticed Dougie entering the rec room and assumed he was there all along with Patrick and had just walked into things on his way out, the opposite direction to the Church.

THE SINGLE LIFE

Molly and Elizabeth couldn't wait for the following Friday night to visit the Phoenix Singles Club; they had talked about it all week. On their first visit the previous Friday, they had drawn the attention of several good-looking men who had bought them drinks before the two had to leave to pick up the children. They had only intended to stay for an hour, but they were having so much fun it was two hours later when they made their way back to Molly's house. Flo hadn't minded as she had been asleep and hadn't even realised they were late returning. The children all had a good time too. Maggie and Lizzie were so shattered the next day after their late night that they slept in for the first time that Elizabeth could remember.

Elizabeth had told the children they could only play in the garden that weekend as she did not intend any more police visits, and they had to earn her trust back. Elizabeth had a quiet Saturday morning and was relaxing when she saw something passing by the window. It seemed strange because it appeared to go down from the top of the window to the bottom, like a big ball. Tutting, she went outside to see what the girls were doing, thinking they must be kicking a ball against the wall above the window and expecting it to break at any moment. Muttering, she opened the door saying, "Can't I have a minute's peace without having to come and tell you off?"

Elizabeth looked at Lizzie standing in front of the window. Then she followed her eyes to the bedroom window, where she saw Maggie just about to lower what looked like a cat in a cage.

145

"What the hell is going on?" demanded Elizabeth before ordering Maggie to get down the stairs.

When Maggie heard her mother's voice, she darted her head back inside, but it was too late. She had been seen. Reluctantly she came downstairs to face the music, carrying the cat in the wire fruit bowl. It meowed loudly as she released it outside. Elizabeth wanted to laugh. It was all so bizarre. Instead, she put her hands on her hips and demanded an explanation of their actions. "We were practising rescuing the cat in case the house ever caught on fire," came Maggie's answer.

'Sometimes I wonder if you act deliberately stupid or you really are. If the house was on fire and we were upstairs, do you really think we would be trying to locate the fruit basket to rescue the cat, or do you think that we would be desperately trying to find a way to save each other?" Scolded Elizabeth.

"It's ok; I know where the fruit basket is now; we don't have to look for it." Replied Maggie.

"God gives me strength; I should ground you both for a month. It's the police one week and then the cat being dangled out of an upstairs bedroom window. It just never ends; I dread to think what you will do next. Can you imagine any man wanting to marry me and take on two delinquents?"

Maggie pulled a face at this, and Elizabeth ordered her inside for the rest of the day. Although that punished her too because she knew she would not have peace if Maggie was bored, Lizzie would at least sit quietly. Elizabeth wanted to sit and daydream about the compliments and smiles received the previous evening. She was in two minds about letting Maggie run wild, and if she ended up in Borstal, at least then she wouldn't have to keep her in check; someone else could do it for a change. Ultimately, Elizabeth couldn't bear the thought of continually telling Maggie to sit down, be quiet, and stop doing that, so

THE PRICE OF SIMPLICITY

she told the children to get their shoes on; they were going for a walk. Elizabeth said aloud, "There is no rest for the wicked." Elizabeth wondered if she had been terrible in her previous life because she never seemed to get any rest at the weekend.

Elizabeth decided to walk on Plover Road towards the Clock Tower and then on Acre Street to Lindley. They took a detour up the snicket, and under the fairy bridge, the lane was always filled with green wishing stones. They all made wishes that would never come true but were good fun. As they walked along, they knew the orphanage was on the other side of the wall. All Elizabeth had to do was look at Maggie, then nod towards the orphanage. Maggie would know she was making a surreptitious threat. One of Lizzie's friends lived in the orphanage and had told Maggie and Lizzie how awful it was, and they were secretly afraid that they may be sent there if things got too bad. They walked to the shops at the end of the road and then turned around. On the way back, Maggie said she knew a secret place on Plover Road that no one else knew about. Elizabeth asked her how 'SHE' knew about it, but Maggie shrugged and said, "I just do."

Maggie said they needed to climb the gate and walk up the field; they would be surprised when they reached the top. Elizabeth asked if this was private land, and Maggie said, "No, because she knew about it, so it couldn't be private." At the top, to Elizabeth's amazement, there was a pond, and she could see fish in abundance. They all watched them for some time before heading to the end of the Plover and across onto Wellington Street to see if Elizabeth's mother was back from her usual day out in town.

Margaret had just gotten off the bus from Huddersfield. She appeared at the top of the field as Elizabeth, Maggie, and Lizzie exited the passageway. Margaret's face lit up when she saw them and quickened her pace; Maggie and Lizzie ran up to meet her, checking her bag for sweets.

When they were all inside and settled, Elizabeth started telling her mother about the big fish pond that Maggie had shown them. Margaret had heard about it and said, "You are lucky the gamekeeper missed you; he could have had you prosecuted for trespassing. That would have been another weekend been interviewed by the police." As Margaret said it, she pursed her lips and nodded, affirming her belief.

Elizabeth once again felt like the failing mother and sighed deeply. In her head, she said, "Roll on Friday." This sparked her to ask her mother if she would babysit the following Friday whilst Elizabeth and Molly from work went out. Vera had finally left to go live in Meltham, and Margaret had her house to herself again.

"Where are you going?" inquired her mother.

But Elizabeth played it down and said she was just going around to Molly's for adult time without the children; she needed a break. Margaret wasn't impressed with her reasoning but agreed to have them. "What time will you be back, or will it be another drunken episode like the last time you went out with Robert Duffy?"

"Elizabeth cringed but said it wouldn't be late; she may even be able to work on Saturday morning if her mother would have the kids all night."

This seemed to appease Margaret, and she agreed to have them hoping they would be staying all night; it was rare that Maggie would stay out and leave her mother; she was still very protective of Elizabeth even though she drove her to despair.

Elizabeth could have skipped home a whole evening to herself when she dropped them off at her mother's. It would be bliss, and she had been offered the chance to work on Saturday

THE PRICE OF SIMPLICITY

morning, so she wasn't lying. She would decide later in the week if she wanted the extra work, the money would be helpful, but the chance to stay in bed and not have to make the girl's breakfast was a luxury she didn't often get.

Friday nights at the Phoenix Club quickly became an exciting routine, a vibrant escape from the monotony of everyday life. They soon had a sense of belonging, familiar with most members, and relaxed in their company. They were no longer the odd ones, devoid of husbands, everyone here was single, and nobody looked down on them. They revelled in the company of newfound friends, forming connections that felt like long-lost kinship. They soon signed up to go on day trips, where they could take the children and still have other adults to talk to.

One such excursion to Chester Zoo brought an unexpected twist. Molly had to cancel at the last minute, leaving Elizabeth alone to take the children on this adventure. Elizabeth lacked the confidence she had when she and Molly did things together. She was happy when Leon, a charismatic Polish immigrant with an intense demeanour, seized the opportunity to become her companion for the day. Laced with a thick accent and broken English, Elizabeth had to move close to him to hear what he said.

As they strolled through the zoo, Leon's enthusiasm was infectious. He marvelled at the majestic creatures with the fervour of a child, relishing the wonder mirrored in Elizabeth's children's eyes. Leon carried their lunch bag, playing the role of a caring protector, making Elizabeth feel at ease in his company.

When lunch arrived, they settled at a picnic table, the children eagerly devouring their meal. Leon, ever the thoughtful one, unveiled a peculiar dark green liquid and suggested Elizabeth try it. His eyes bore into her, his tone serious as he spoke of its miraculous health benefits. A sense of unease washed over Elizabeth as he mentioned making the elixir for a friend who had tragically passed away, hinting that the potion might have

149

extended his life if he hadn't died.

Caught off guard, Elizabeth struggled to find a gracious way to decline, her mind racing to find an excuse. She stumbled over her words, ultimately succumbing to the pressure, promising to try the elixir at home. But it was Maggie's innocent remark cutting through the tension, inadvertently providing an escape. Hungry and oblivious to the situation, the young girl offered to eat her mother's sandwiches if she had the slime for lunch.

Relief washed over Elizabeth's face, grateful for her daughter's interruption. Sternly, she reprimanded Maggie for her greediness, just thankful she could focus the attention on disciplining Maggie and away from what might be a deadly poison. Maggie muttered a half-hearted apology, silenced by her mother's warning glare.

At that moment, Elizabeth realised that the single life could be filled with trepidation, and she would have to ensure she kept her wits about her to avoid possible unseen traps in the future. As the day continued, having avoided drinking Leon's magic potion, Elizabeth relaxed. The children were having a great day out, and she was grateful that the club had given her this opportunity to mix and not feel alone and embarrassed.

Although Molly and Elizabeth had casually dated a few of the men from the club, they started meeting up with the same two men each week, and the four became good friends. All four were forming serious relationships. They stopped going to the Phoenix Club and started driving out to country pubs as a foursome, sometimes seeing each other without the other couple being around. Molly's man, Bob, had met her children, and they all got on well. Now it was Elizabeth's turn to introduce Richard to Molly and Lizzie.

THINGS ARE CHANGING

When Chester was eventually found, hours had gone by, and not much was left of his face. The flesh was torn from his lips, nose and cheeks by the voracity of this animal in its bid to escape. The rat had burrowed through the only soft surface it could find with sharp claws and teeth; the rat quickly gnawed into Chester's mouth and fled from the back of his neck. Luckily for Chester, he was dead before the rat got to work on him. But what was left for his brother to see was beyond any nightmare.

Kieran and Chester had been a formidable force and the unlikely custodians of order behind the bars of the prison wing. No one would dare to do anything without their official approval. Now that order had been disrupted, one of the strong links had been shattered, leaving a 'Lone Wolf' behind. This lone wolf was now more vulnerable than he had ever been in his life. Kieran and Chester had a bond that could never be broken but would ultimately lead to their downfall.

Kieran had screamed when he first saw Chester's chewed and deformed face, then cried like a child, sobbing on his bed with his door closed firmly. As Kieran's priest, Patrick would inevitably have to knock on the door at some point to offer his condolences and listen to Kieran voice his sorrow. The way that Kieran handled this episode would be duly noted by all the up-and-coming gang leaders in the wing, waiting to take control.

They would not hesitate to destroy the weakened Kieran to rise up the ranks; business is business in the prisoner's world. Like an alpha male wolf, he is quickly taken down when he comes across a stronger or more ferocious opponent. His choices become limited, taking over a weaker pack or becoming a scavenger.

In normal circumstances, the prison environment challenges every aspect of grieving, and Patrick, along with everyone else, realised that Kieran would soon snap out of his melancholy. It would be replaced with an eruption of fury. Somebody would pay for Chester's death; more than likely, a lot of people would pay for Chester's death.

The Church had been closed down for the investigation, and Patrick and anyone else who used the Church were interviewed. Chester's cell was being searched first, and a post-mortem was scheduled for the following day. This was going to be a lengthy process; the whereabouts of the whole wing were being established and corroborated.

Patrick needed to gain access to Kieran's cell to speak to him before the final lockdown of the day, and knowing his mood would be unstable, Patrick asked the Governor for an escort to determine the safety of entering the cell. It was unknown if Kieran's temperament would be highly volatile, explosive, or docile.

Luckily, when Patrick entered the cell, Kieran was still lying on the bed, rocking himself and saying Chester's name. Patrick did his best to talk to Kieran, but nothing would break through the deep sorrow that Kieran was dealing with. Patrick told him he would call by first thing in the morning when Kieran had time to process his grief. Patrick left quickly, relieved that he would not have to deal with this torment tonight.

When he returned to his cell, Patrick wondered briefly if Dougie

THE PRICE OF SIMPLICITY

knew anything about what had happened in the Church and made a mental note to speak to him privately the next day. Today had been a big shock for everyone, and the person responsible would soon change things on the wing, and it was yet unknown if that was a good or bad thing.

The next day when the cells were unlocked, the guards had doubled in number in preparation for the potential consequences of Chester's death and Kieran's reaction to it. Kieran had refused to go to breakfast, giving Patrick a little time to speak to Dougie before he had to go and console Kieran. Dougie was not a blabbermouth, and Patrick knew it may take him a long time to draw the information out of Dougie even if Dougie was aware of what had happened. Patrick remembered that Dougie had arrived late to the rec room. He assumed he had been playing cards or chatting with Joey, who he had befriended over the last few months. Joey had a lot of time for Dougie, knowing what it was like to walk with a deformity and the stick you could get from the other inmates. Joey had learnt to ignore the constant ribbing and could usually give as good as he got, but his toes were his only abnormality.

Dougie was afflicted in many ways, his speech being the worst and most obvious defect, causing others to see him as deaf, dumb and blind and often reminding him of his shortcomings. If they had known he was responsible for the death of one of the fiercest men on the wing, they might have looked twice at Dougie and seen him more for what he was becoming.

While Patrick was eating his breakfast with Dougie, Joey joined them. Patrick tried to ask innocently if they had played cards, pool, or some other game yesterday afternoon. Joey answered first, telling Patrick he had been in the library looking over some facts about the best musical hit that has a prison as a theme. He said it was to solve an argument he had been having with one of his associates, "I said it was Elvis Presley's 'Jail House Rock', and he said it was Johnny Cash's 'I walk the line'. I wanted to know which sold the most copies, but I still need to find out. Why do you ask?"

Patrick turned and looked at Dougie, and in that second, he knew it had been Dougie who had killed Chester, and this was the worst news he could have heard. Patrick knew Dougie had done this deed for him out of misguided love and respect. Dougie stared back at Patrick without saying a word. Patrick desperately needed to speak to Dougie alone to find the entire truth and, if need be, establish an alibi for him.

Dougie fell into a little researched category. He had exceptional ability and disability. Dougie was gifted in some way but had extreme developmental challenges. In real terms, those less gifted were not up to the challenge of understanding or accepting the freak who stood in front of them, barely able to speak but with a hidden IQ off the chart. His tormentors usually were kids who struggled to attain a grade recognised for their age group and spent most of their school years outside the Principal's office or wagging school. Dougie's genius had never been realised because there had never been anyone exceptional enough to assess him. And, instead trusted their visual instincts that were not honed to spot extremes of any classification.

Dougie's disabilities had always overshadowed his ability. Had Dougie ever been assessed, he would undoubtedly have scored in a superior range in visual-spatial thinking, including perception, analysis and synthesis.

But the lumbering, almost mute immobile that staggered into a room banging into people was criticised, scolded and harangued by his family, peers, teachers and even doctors since he was old enough to be in the public eye. Dougie's self-esteem, anxiety and frustration deeply harmed Dougie, causing years of adolescent depression, leading him to be selectively mute and poorly performing in most areas of school life. Dougie's intense personality, fighting internally to understand what was happening in his head and the extreme violence and abuse he received from the day he was born made life severely tricky. As a coping strategy, Dougie learnt to hide in plain sight, become invisible and avoid being a target for the pleasure of those less aware.

Dougie's mind was intense. He had no opportunity to demonstrate this trait, so instead of exhibiting extreme bouts of violence and behavioural difficulties at school that he rarely attended, Dougie became fixated on saving his sister and mother. He began training to build muscle and endurance to the point of obsession.

Once Dougie's intense fascination was to a standard that Dougie considered adequate, he executed his plan. Still, he had not yet learnt how to end the obsession and STOP. In the case of his stepfather, not much remained that was recognisable when Dougie had finished. Similar to his planned execution of Chester.

Dougie had become obsessed with Patrick since his arrival in the penitentiary. He had become obsessed with finding a weakness in Patrick's tormentors, i.e. Kieran but mostly Chester, that he could use to his advantage to eliminate them from Patrick's life. In Dougie's immature but clever mind, Dougie was saving Patrick from any further threat. Still, he had not considered its effect on the prison population he had no control over.

Patrick was aware that at some point, Kieran would start to question how the murder, which must have been planned, happened so conveniently and seamlessly in Patrick's Church. Even a fool would need to seek clarification from the man in charge of where the murder of his brother had taken place. A brother who meant more to Kieran than anything on Earth. Kieran recognised Chester had problems that he cared for and had taken care of since Chester was a small child. Kieran would cover up all Chester's indiscretions. Kieran took care of Chester and not their parents, who were violent alcoholics. Kieran discovered very early in Chester's life that he lacked empathy, remorse or guilt when he harmed, maimed and later killed things out of curiosity or revenge. Chester was a pathological liar with no friends and was feared by his peers and teachers. When their drunken parents died in a horrific fire, Kieran knew it was a deliberate act by Chester when he found him hiding and giggling as he watched his mother's face blister and then ignite from a peephole he had made before lighting the fire and locking his parents in the room. Kieran held Chester not to comfort him but to try and hide that he was sexually aroused and excited by their parent's death, not distraught like he should have been as a ten-year-old child.

They spent the next six years in one after another foster home. Chester always frightened the carers so much they had to be moved on for everyone's safety. The only person who Chester loved or listened to was his brother Kieran. And with such a vast responsibility, Chester was the only person Kieran was ever free to love. Kieran had once fallen in love with a beautiful, innocent young girl he was devoted to. He soon recognised that Chester was jealous, and Kieran became frightened for her safety. Kieran tried to end the relationship knowing that Chester would eventually hurt her for coming between them, but it was too late. Chester hid and watched the girl as she spent time with her family on a Church picnic that Kieran and Chester had been invited to. Chester drowned the girl holding her under the water and laughing as she splashed and fought him desperately to save her life. Kieran had had to cover up the murder claiming he saw her trapped beneath a log and did everything he could to save her. Chester had actually thought Kieran would be pleased with him, and this was when Kieran understood that he would never be able to have a relationship beyond his brother Chester.

When Kieran awoke the following morning for a nanosecond, he forgot about Chester. Then the memory flooded back into

THE PRICE OF SIMPLICITY

his brain, crashing, banging and slamming into his heart and head. Kieran had a migraine. He suffered from extreme remorse and grief; losing Chester was like losing a child. Kieran should have protected his brother better, kept a keener eye on him, and reined him in more often. But Chester was a grown man, and Kieran knew he couldn't control him; Chester made his own decisions, and sometimes his ideas made a lot of sense, like getting Patrick to lead the Church so they could run the racket through legitimately leaving Patrick responsible. Patrick would be the first person Kieran would speak to about his brother's murder in Patrick's Church. He must know something. He would kill the fucking priest if he found out he was a part of it, and it wouldn't be a quick death, either. Kieran was starting to get angry and vengeful; time to get out of bed and start work.

He made a request to speak to the Governor. He prepared arrangements to bribe the guards to find any information discovered during the investigation.

FACING THE MUSIC

As Patrick walked along the corridor, he saw that Kieran's cell door stood ajar and could hear the shouting getting louder as he approached. He took a deep breath and knocked on the door. Dougie had followed Patrick and stood watching on guard to protect his saviour if anything should kick off. Inside the cell, there were three of Kieran's men receiving instructions to "Find the wanker who killed my brother and find him fast. Somebody knows something; a crime of this magnitude would take more than one man to plan and execute. There will be a reward paid to the man who brings me the guilty fucker, and I want them alive. I will plan to deal with them once I know the details."

Kieran dismissed the men and then turned his attention towards Patrick, pushing his face so far forward it was almost touching Patrick's. Kieran hissed into Patrick's face, "Who did it?"

Patrick knew that Kieran was desperate and desperate men never thought rationally, just quickly and instinctively; Kieran was reacting primarily with his heart and not his head. For the moment, Patrick had the advantage; his thoughts were calculated and not irrational, but he was still aware of the emotional element and the impact on others. As Patrick had laid in bed last night thinking about the situation, and Dougie's possible involvement, he believed that no one would suspect Dougie of being capable of a crime that had taken time to plan.

Patrick remained calm as he looked at Kieran, confidently

asked him to sit down, and, with composure and assurance, said, "Let's analyse the situation strategically before jumping to conclusions. Many faces on this wing await you to go berserk and start running amok. When you burn out, they will quietly step into your shoes, and you may lose everything."

Kieran sat down and listened to Patrick as an equal. Unlike all the rest of his team, Kieran knew Patrick was not in this for financial gain or to overthrow Kieran. Patrick was doing his job as a priest, and it was just what Kieran needed, a man he could trust. Kieran felt a pang of guilt when he recognised that this had never been possible when Chester was alive. They slowly began to talk and make a list of anyone who may benefit from Chester's death. Kieran had to admit the list was longer than he would have liked. Still, they could think about each viable suspect and eliminate them from the list methodically. Kieran needed allies, not enemies, and by working things out logically and calmly, he was presenting himself as a strong, intelligent leader and not just a strong-armed thug. Never before had Kieran thought about his business in such a way; he had always ruled by fear and intimidation, but now realised working with an educated ally opened up far more possibilities for the future.

Patrick was playing for time, and his plan was working. He left Kieran to make the list while he went to find Dougie. As Patrick had suspected, Dougie was waiting outside, and they walked back to Patrick's cell. Nobody would think twice about the two of them going to the cell; Dougie was known as Patrick's ward and was aware that they spent time platonically together.

In prison, eyes and ears are everywhere, constantly trying to gain information they can use to their advantage. As Patrick and Dougie entered the cell, Patrick put his finger to his lips to let Dougie know not to say anything whilst he checked for eavesdroppers. All the cons were on high alert to find any snippet of information regarding Chester's death to pass on to

Kieran in the hope of some favour, so privacy was paramount. Speaking in whispers, Patrick began questioning Dougie and gradually discovered what had happened. As Dougie revealed the intricacies of what had occurred beneath the stage in the Church, Patrick was horrified by Dougie's revelations. Still, he admired the man for his planning and patience. Patrick had begun to suspect Dougie's intentional, tactical mind weeks before the murder. When he had found him carefully amending all orders for any item that contained drugs or contraband to Kieran's name. Dougie could barely write but had practised painstakingly for weeks to write Kieran's signature.

Patrick realised now why Dougie had come into the rec room but then created so much fuss as he went to use the toilet. Dougie had given himself a perfect alibi. He knew when people in the rec room were interviewed, they would remember the 'oaf', being there and banging about as usual. Patrick would also swear that Dougie had been there with him, which Kieran would hear, eliminating either of them from any inquiries.

Even though nearly everyone on the wing was trying desperately to find out any information, much to the amazement and annoyance of Kieran Delaney, nobody was saying anything of any use. It was now public knowledge that Chester had tried to get under the stage in the Church, where he had been trapped by somebody waiting for him. It was speculated that it would have taken at least two people to lure and hold him. The mark on Chester's neck was vivid and would have taken extreme strength to enforce. It was still uncertain if the rat in the hole that held Chester's head was incidental, but it was suspected that it was. The offending rat was long gone when Chester was found, so no analysis could be conducted.

Patrick had met up with Kieran daily to review what had been gleaned from guards on his payroll and those cons that remained loyal to him. The list had gradually become shorter, and it had been a relief when some of the inmates had been cleared of suspicion. The ones that remained were the ones who were also waiting to take over from Kieran when he next showed a chink in his armour or the person responsible was found. They would then either become allies or enemies of the obviously powerful adversary that dared to take on the Delaney's without the allegiance of one of the other top families.

After the list had been whittled down to three, maybe four remaining gangs whose whereabouts were not affirmed, it became a situation where there would be a standoff. Kieran currently controlled the wing with the perception that he had more control over events in prison than the staff and that order may only be maintained if his leadership was not jeopardised.

Kieran had started to talk about war; this frightened Patrick, who was well aware of the injuries and loss of innocent lives that the impact of this backlash would have on the inmates and staff of the prison. Kieran was certain Chester's killer was among the few remaining names, and it had gotten to the point where he couldn't care less if others died in the aftermath of a deadlock. A clear leader would emerge, and Kieran had already started gathering his troops with promises of large payouts for anyone who remained loyal throughout. Threats were made to anyone defecting at any time until this was over.

After one particularly harrowing meeting with Kieran, Patrick left his cell looking defeated and stripped of any energy to continue. Dougie, as always, was waiting for him and steered him towards the chess board in the rec room. Patrick couldn't understand Dougie's intention knowing he could not play the game. Then Dougie began to elaborate on his strategical thinking using the chess pieces to explain rather than words that could be overheard, especially words that Dougie struggled with.

Dougie pointed to the King and said, "Governor." He then

indicated a Queen saying, "Kieran", and swept his hand over all the pawns that stood with the Queen. He then pointed to the other Queen and said, "Enemies." Dougie then lifted Kieran off the table and said, "Checkmate."

Patrick was amazed at this analogy and realised what Dougie said was true. If Kieran was removed from the game by the Governor, then peace would prevail. He looked across at Dougie and shook Dougie's hand, saying, "Thank you, Dougie. You solved this prison's most significant problem with three chess pieces. Patrick decided to take the same analogy to the Governor and let him work it out for himself. That night Patrick wrote the scenario down in the shape of a story to tell the Governor tomorrow. This way, his conscience was clear he had betrayed no one; he had merely written an account for the Governor, with all the dilemmas of chess, a game he knew the Governor to be fond of.

Patrick's story

"In the dark underbelly of a prison, a thrilling and dangerous game of power unfolded. Patrick was a pawn, a prisoner with a haunting past. He was trapped in a web spun by the merciless gang leader, Kieran Delaney, King of the Wing and his ruthless brother, Chester, the mighty Queen, by his side. The two had a powerful team of chess pieces to manipulate. Patrick was forced into the treacherous world of prison gangs, bound by fear and became their Bishop, a substantial part of the set.

Kieran's fury knew no bounds as the news of Chester's brutal demise rippled through the prison. His thirst for vengeance consumed him, and he launched a merciless search for the elusive perpetrator. Unbeknownst to Kieran, his violent outbursts against his pawns only served to sow seeds of rebellion within his ranks. Ambitious and cunning gang leaders, acting like opposing knights and bishops, saw an opportunity to seize power, sensing Kieran's vulnerability.

Kieran's Bishop, Patrick, burdened by the weight of impending bloodshed and anarchy, realised the dire consequences ahead if Kieran remained King on the hypothetical chess board; or within the prison walls. Recognising the urgency, he clandestinely arranged a secret meeting with the Governor, revealing the potential horrors that awaited if action wasn't taken swiftly.

The Governor faced with the gravity of the situation, contemplated the precarious future of the prison. Acknowledging the wisdom in Patrick's words, he understood the necessity of removing Kieran from the equation. With a steely resolve, the Governor initiated the wheels of change, setting in motion a series of covert manoeuvrers to arrange Kieran's transfer.

As the chessboard of power shifted, alliances were forged, and unseen forces plotted behind the prison walls. Patrick, driven by a desire for redemption and the salvation of innocent lives, played his part in a dangerous game determining the fate of the prison's future.

As the wheels of fate turned, the prison trembled with anticipation. The countdown had begun, and the race against time to remove Kieran from the equation would shape the destiny of all entangled in this perilous web of power and deceit.

In the shadows, a glimmer of hope emerged, fuelled by the audacity of two men determined to bring order to the chaos. But with every move, danger loomed, and the stakes grew higher.

Amidst the looming darkness, the battle for control raged on, with the clash of wills, cunning strategies, and sacrifices that would leave an indelible mark on the lives of everyone involved. Redemption and survival hung in the balance, and only the most daring and resolute would emerge victorious."

Patrick had worked hard to make the story sound like a 'War of the Worlds' drama that needed someone stronger, wiser, and more astute to halt the chaos and regain an order of semblance.

Kieran used to have goals and a clear direction of preferred results; now, it was the personification of chaos and 'Gotham City' needed the Governor to rule. The flattery worked; the Governor looked up as realisation hit, and he shook Patrick's hand. Wise words Father; now all we need is the hand of God to work with us to delay the aftermath left behind by 'The Joker' Batman's sworn enemy and a homicidal maniac.

When Patrick left the Governor's office, he felt safer than he had in a long time. He still had to humour Kieran and keep him onside and trusting of his council. Still, he hoped the advice he had passed on to the Governor would be implemented sooner rather than later. It was all thanks to the ingenious mind of the most unlikely character on the wing. What a shame Dougie had never been given a chance to realise his potential;. However, he was still young, and the damage done to Dougie was unlikely to offer him any respite from the impairments already in place. If Patrick was released, his next calling would be to work with victims of childhood abuse, and having Dougie as an advisor on the scheme would be gold as far as Patrick was concerned.

MAGGIE

Monday, the fifteenth of February nineteen seventy was a momentous day in the life of Maggie Ryan. It was the day she turned twelve, and decimalisation entered circulation in the UK. The week before her birthday, Maggie had two boyfriends named Graham. They were equally obsessed with the highly spirited, volatile, outspoken Maggie.

At school, she was friends with them both; she would have preferred it if they would accept that she could have two boyfriends at once. They had very different personalities, likes, and dislikes; she liked them for their differences, seeing the advantages of each of them. Mashed together, they were perfect. But, both Grahams tried to outdo the other to make her want them more, and this rivalry was getting on Maggie's nerves.

Graham C was kind-hearted and gave her things from his collections, largely dull, like a large conker he treasured or a bird feather he had found. But, what Maggie did find exciting about him, apart from his racing bike he was teaching her to ride, was that he would tell her stories taken from the classics he had read. Maggie found it more exciting than anything she had ever heard before. She longed to be one of the characters that seemed to be on infinite adventures where they always became triumphant. The characters never seemed sad or didn't know what to do; they just got on with things and always won their adversaries. But Graham C could be too steady and boring, and even though he was interesting because he knew so much, Maggie found him unexciting.

Maggie was spending more and more time with her other boyfriend, Graham K. He was good-looking, always up to mischief, and made her laugh until her sides ached. He was wicked and daring, and Maggie was enthralled with what he might do next.

Maggie had kissed Graham K more than once and had enjoyed it. She knew Graham K was far more mature than her, which she found a little scary, especially when he had asked her to show him her knickers and tried to touch her under her vest. Maggie had been shocked and scared but had liked it too. This was a new phenomenon for her; she didn't know how to stop him or if she should. Her instincts told her it was wrong, but would he think she was a little girl if she said "No?" Maggie was wise enough to know that Graham K would inevitably end up in deep trouble, and if she was with him, she would too.

Maggie had not started developing breasts and wondered what he wanted to touch. She wished she could grow big, round bosoms like some of her friends; it made them look much older than her. But, at the moment, her ribs stood out further than her chest, which was embarrassing now that she had a proper boyfriend like Graham K.

She thought back to a few months ago when she had met him at the High School she had started and remembered he never used to try and touch her. Then they just had fun, teasing people or getting told off in class for misbehaving and talking. Her teacher had told her she was 'skating on thin ice'; Maggie had no idea what that meant but guessed she was close to serious trouble.

Maggie sat with Julie, her best friend, telling her all about how funny Graham K could be and how boring Graham C was in comparison. Maggie pretended to be self-assured and told Julie (who had enormous bosoms) that she let Graham touch her under her vest and that he had seen inside her knickers. He hadn't, but Maggie wanted to make Julie jealous and hoped Julie would think that Maggie was grown up if she was doing adult things. Maggie darednt admit to being scared of Graham; he was so strong when she tried to stop him. Maggie had started trying to avoid being alone with Graham, and he had become more insistent that they go somewhere private. At every opportunity, Maggie knew Graham would try to pin her down and touch her; it was so hard to stop him. The last time he had been very rough with her pushing her against a wall and pulling her knickers down. Luckily a man came around the corner, and Graham jumped back from her. The man shouted at them both, and Maggie pulled up her knickers as fast as she could and ran home, afraid the man would follow her and tell her Mum.

Even at school, Graham was relentlessly following her about, grabbing at her with a deranged look. The teacher had caught him trying to touch her under the desk, pinning her legs against the chair. She had got into trouble, too, and they had both been sent to stand outside the Headmaster's office. Maggie knew her dad would kill Graham if he found out he had been trying to grab her like that. The thought of her Mum, Nanna and Dad finding out filled her with shame.

While standing alone waiting for the Headmaster, Graham tried again to grab her. Without thinking, she returned her fist and punched him in the nose just as the Headmaster's door opened. Blood spurted from Graham's nose, and the Headmaster grabbed Maggie by the arm and dragged her inside his room while he tried to stem the blood flow and ensure Graham was ok.

Graham was taken to Matron, and the Headmaster returned to speak to Maggie. "What is going on between you and Graham? Is there some sort of problem? I will not tolerate violence in this school, especially by a girl. It is time you started acting like a lady instead of a female thug. You are getting quite a reputation for your wayward, out-of-control behaviour. I think it is time to get your parents involved."

Those were the words Maggie was dreading, and she knew she would have to do something drastic to ensure her Mum didn't receive the letter home from school. Maggie slunk out of the office and back to class; everyone looked at her as she walked in with her head down. She wanted to run away but couldn't think of anywhere to run to. Besides which, February was too cold to run away from home. This was going to be her worst birthday ever.

When Graham returned to class, he glared across at Maggie, and she was glad he had fallen out with her. Even though she knew she was in serious trouble, at least she didn't have to fight Graham off any more.

After school, Maggie ran home instead of waiting outside to walk home with Graham, hoping to avoid seeing him. She ran to Nanna's house across the field and let herself in with the key under the stone. Maggie ran upstairs, threw herself on Nanna's bed and cried; everything seemed to be going wrong again, and Maggie had no idea how to fix things. She jumped up and, in frustration, threw her shoe against the wall. But instead of hitting the wall, it clipped the window shattering the glass and letting in a gust of icy cold air.

Maggie stared at the shattered glass, biting her lip and swearing. She tiptoed over to the window and gazed onto the field, knowing her Nanna would be home any moment, and then she would be in real trouble.

Maggie heard her Nanna crunching over the broken glass and saying, "Oh my God, what's happened?"

She heard Nanna open the door and shout, "Who's there? Is anybody there?"
Maggie called, "It's me, Nan; I'm upstairs."

Margaret raced upstairs expecting the worst, thinking they must have been burgled and Maggie had come home to find the carnage. Margaret looked at Maggie's face and knew she had been the one to break the glass. Maggie started before Margaret could ask her, "I broke the window, Nan. When I came home from school, I ran upstairs because I thought I heard someone. When I looked out the window, I thought I saw a shadow move, so I threw my shoe at it. But no one was there, and the window smashed."

Margaret didn't know what to believe but thought the story was too far-fetched to be made up. She could imagine a child coming home, being frightened by a noise, and reacting before thinking. "You shouldn't have come upstairs if you thought someone was here, Maggie; that is dangerous. What if someone had been here? You might be dead now?"

Maggie knew her lies had worked, but she felt guilty she had created a cost for her Nanna and was worried her Nanna would be cold with the broken window. "Can you sleep at our house until the window is fixed, Nan? I don't want you to be cold tonight. And, I especially don't want a burglar to get you if he sneaks in the broken window."

Nanna said they would have to hurry down to Mr Smith, the joiner and see if he could board it up until he could fix it. "God knows how much this is going to cost, though?"

Again Maggie felt terrible for what she had done; she knew her Nanna didn't have any spare money, especially for the window that she had broken. Maggie sighed and followed her Nan down the road to see Mr Smith.

As luck would have it, Mr Smith was working late and agreed to come and board the window up until the next day. He said he might have a pane of glass in the shed the same size as all the

SHELAGH TAYLOR

houses on this terrace. Frank Smith had fixed many of them over the years and was well stocked, being the only glacier in the area. He even said he might be able to do it a bit cheaper as she had been through a lot lately, and he had never had a chance to pay his respects to her brother Jack when he died.

THINGS GO FROM BAD TO WORSE

Kieran's behaviour was becoming increasingly irrational; he was getting paranoid about not finding those responsible for his brother Chester's death. He needed to find and punish the guilty, or he would start to lose face amongst the prison population as not having the power to control the wing.

Each day he had a final meeting with his team of thugs. Each time they told him they had no firm evidence of who had been responsible, Kieran systematically picked off and punished his own men, thinking they were working against him. Yet, so far, no one had spoken up, even under torture, to make them any the wiser to the possible culprit or culprits. This was not usual in prison; having secrets was almost impossible, and everybody had a price and would sell their own granny for a pack of tobacco. His members had beaten, maimed and hospitalised many prisoners in their search for the truth but had still to find those responsible.

After two weeks of torturing his own men, removing fingers or toes, ears, and one, even an eye in search of a traitor, his own men began to turn. They were steadily drifting towards other big names on the wing, and Kieran gained more enemies than he could handle. The Governor was racing against time to have Kieran moved to another facility where he would be safer, and so would the rest of the prison population at this facility.

After a vivid dream where Patrick had nailed Chester to a crucifix in the church, Kieran was convinced that it was a message from his dead brother to the real culprit he sent for Patrick.

Dougie walked behind Patrick and waited as Patrick entered Kieran's cell. Everyone could hear Kieran screaming at Patrick that Chester had sent a message to warn him about Patrick while sleeping. "I know that you are the FUCKING CUNT, that murdered my brother. I don't know why I trusted you so long, Chester never trusted you and warned me to get rid of you when he was alive, but I wouldn't listen. Now he's dead, and you are up and down the place as if you own it. Well, your time has come."

As quick as a flash, Kieran produced a knife from his waistband and lunged at Patrick. Dougie had listened to Kieran screaming his threats to Patrick and inched closer. Usually, Kieran's men would have stopped him, but they stood back, staring at the man whose eyes had glazed over. Dougie walked into the cell silently. Kieran hung over Patrick, stabbing him with the knife; Patrick tried in vain to fight him off, holding his arm and aiming blows towards Kieran's face. Dougie crept up behind Kieran and in the confined space that wouldn't allow for Kieran to turn around as he was sandwiched between Patrick and Dougie. Dougie grabbed the knife and plunged it deep into Kieran's neck. Blood gushed from the severed artery and rained onto the helpless Patrick below Kieran. By now, unaware of what he was doing, Dougie continued stabbing Kieran repeatedly in the neck. Kieran's head sagged, almost severed, when guards rushed into the room and dragged Dougie off Kieran, who slumped atop Patrick.

The dominant gangs on the wing swooped to take over the vacant position provided by Kieran's absence; even though he was still alive, Kieran would never be the same robust adversary he had been upon entering Wakefield Prison.

THE PRICE OF SIMPLICITY

As Kieran was rushed to hospital with life-threatening injuries, discussions were underway to determine who would enforce order amongst the prisoners. Patrick was also severely injured and needed immediate hospital treatment. Still, luckily for him, unlike Kieran, his injuries were not life-threatening. Dougie was taken away for questioning, but for the first time in his life went as a hero to his fellow inmates.

WEDDING BELLS

Elizabeth and Richard's relationship had reached the point where marriage was the logical next step. They saw each other every weekend and introduced the children. Still, they had not spent much time together as a blended family. Richard had three girls that lived with him full-time. Debbie was ten and the same age as Lizzie, then two younger girls, Katrina, nine and Anne, nearly eight.

Margaret first met Richard on Friday night when she babysat for Maggie and Lizzie. Elizabeth walked into Margaret's house with Richard in tow; Margaret took one look at him and realised he was drunk. He slurred his hello's, and Margaret instantly disliked him and trusted him even less. When Maggie saw her mum, she asked if she could go home, but Margaret said, "No."

An argument erupted that became a slanging match. Finally, Elizabeth grabbed Maggie's arm and pulled her out of the house. Elizabeth was embarrassed that her mother had made such a fuss about the man she was romantically entangled with. That alone was enough to spur her on to rush into a marriage that was not really suitable. Elizabeth was cross that her mother had not instantly liked Richard and decided to cut her nose to spite her face showing her mother she would do as she wanted and didn't need her anymore.

Richard couldn't care less; he was glad that he would not have to deal with a dominating 'Mother-in-Law' as he could easily pull the wool over the naïve eyes of Elizabeth. Richard needed a compliant woman who would bring money into the house, look after his children, cook, wash, and clean. It was a bonus that she was good-looking. He intended to carry on doing exactly what he wanted, and being married to Elizabeth would make it a lot easier. Elizabeth didn't know that when Richard spent the night at her house, he left his three children alone and did not see a problem with this. His children's school started asking questions when they talked about going to bed when they wanted because their dad was not there at the weekend.

Elizabeth had been to Richard's house once. She knew it needed to be more significant for a family of seven if they married and moved there, but there were no other viable choices. Elizabeth had suggested they buy a bigger house, and Richard had been all for it until he realised she had less money than him. Although he owned the house, it was jointly owned with his ex-wife; selling it and giving her half would leave them even worse off. The house was a front-end terrace with one bedroom, a box room and an attic. There was only one living area. The cooker, washing machine, and bathroom were in the cellar, which flooded every time it rained. Still, they had no choice. Neither of them had any savings, and as Richard would hardly ever be there, it didn't worry him. "We'll manage; it will be like camping. The girls can all squash in together, and we will have the attic room."

Elizabeth was determined to make things work, so they ignored that five girls sharing a bedroom would cause much trouble.

Elizabeth told Molly about the argument and said marriage had been discussed with Richard. Elizabeth was excited to be planning a wedding, even if it had to be done cheaply. Molly offered to make sandwiches at her house after the registry office wedding as a present. Elizabeth said that Richard was saving up for a wedding ring for her, but it seemed to be taking forever. Molly suggested Elizabeth buy her own out of the catalogue and pay weekly for it. She knew Richard promised many things but failed to deliver on most of them; he liked to be the big man boasting about what he had and what he had done, but more often than not, these were his fantasies, not reality.

A more pressing matter was Elizabeth's need to organise a method of birth control; at thirty-four, she considered herself far too old to get pregnant and five children was more than enough for anybody. She hadn't needed birth control since leaving Danny, but as she was going to marry Richard, she had let things go further than she should have with him on more than one occasion. Luckily, he was not averse to using Durex, which had served as a temporary measure. But Elizabeth had been fooled once before into trusting the rubber sheath that Danny had filled with holes to give his sperm a fighting chance if God willed it. Never again would she fall for that, not that Richard was a Catholic or wanted any more children.

The first time that Richard slept over in her single bed, spooned together, had been the first time they had made love. She couldn't lay in a bed so close to a man she was in a relationship with without succumbing to his advances; it wouldn't have been fair to tell Richard "No."

So, instead of fighting off his advances, she had allowed them to happen, petrified of the consequences of falling pregnant or rejecting yet another man and ending up alone because of something she had been taught by the Catholic church and her mother. Neither the Catholic Church nor her mother had saved her child, so why should Elizabeth listen to their words. What if they were wrong and she had to spend the rest of her life as a single woman, an 'Old Maid'? The thought frightened her more than anything else.

The sex hadn't been fantastic like she had hoped. In fact, it was rushed and unfulfilling, coupled with the fact that she had laid there worrying about everything whilst it took place, which was not helpful. It had started with groping, her nighty being pulled

THE PRICE OF SIMPLICITY

up, then urgent thrusting and gasping from Richard, and then it was over. Just like that, no fireworks or earth tremors. 'Wham Bam and thank you, Ma'am' Elizabeth lay awake, wondering if Richard had put a condom on. If he did, he must have had it ready; and expected to have sex with her. She wondered if he always carried them around with him and how often he had sex with other people or had bought them just to be with her? Elizabeth knew these were not the thoughts she should be having; she should be basking in the afterglow of sex, something the other, younger members of the mending room talked about every Monday.

Elizabeth had made an appointment after work on Friday at the Princess Royal Family Planning clinic. Sitting in the waiting room, she looked around and suddenly felt old. The waiting room was full of young girls that barely looked sixteen, all chatting and giggling without a care in the world. They had probably already had far more sexual experience than her and wouldn't have laid there worrying when their boyfriend was making love to them; they would have relaxed and had fun.

Finally, it was her turn, and she got up to follow the nurse into a side room where she was told to sit at a desk next to the doctor, who didn't even look up to acknowledge her. He was writing up the notes from the previous patient, and it seemed like forever before he turned his attention to her. She hoped he didn't think she was a woman of easy virtue, having to get sexual protection at her age.

The doctor asked about her name, age and marital status; Elizabeth blushed and explained that she was about to get married and needed birth control to stop pregnancies. She then began telling him about the traumatic births she had endured and how the doctors had advised her never to get pregnant again. He held up his hand to stop her talking and said, "I don't advise the pill for a woman of your age, but the coil will be suitable. Make an appointment to have a coil fitted and take a leaflet explaining the procedure on your way out."

He started writing again as Elizabeth followed the nurse into the waiting room and the front appointment desk. The nurse at the front desk looked up and stared at Elizabeth, who asked for an appointment for the coil fitting. Elizabeth tried to whisper, but the nurse repeated everything she said loudly. Elizabeth was asked when her next period was due and if she usually had a heavy bleed. Cringing, Elizabeth replied she did bleed heavily and her next period was in a week. The nurse said, in that case, we will make the appointment for the week after and proceeded to hand over a bag filled to the brim with condoms, stating, "Here are twenty condoms to keep you going until your appointment in a fortnight, if you need any more just come to this desk and collect them."

Elizabeth was mortified. She felt like every pair of eyes in the room would look at her and think she was a nymphomaniac. She had never felt so embarrassed and hoped this marriage would be worth all this angst. Without turning around, Elizabeth hurried to leave the clinic.

Elizabeth still wasn't speaking to her mother even though Margret still had Lizzie after school every day. Maggie had started going home alone and felt grown up, letting herself into the house with her key. She would usually run upstairs and take out the packet of cigarettes she bought weekly with the money her dad gave her, take one from the pack and re-hide the box in her drawer. Maggie would then go downstairs, sit in her mother's chair, light the cigarette with the matches hidden behind the curtain, and pretend to be a teenager smoking with her feet on the settee arm. Maggie knew her mother was planning on marrying Richard and was glad she would remain the eldest child and wouldn't have to 'Tow-the-line' for an older sibling. She was also pleased that she was leaving Salendine

Nook and the lecherous Graham.

The previous episode had taken an unfortunate turn for Maggie, a warning sign of repercussions that awaited her. Caught in a moment of retaliation, she had resorted to thumping Graham in front of the Headmaster, Mr Spencer. However, to her dismay, the Headmaster overlooked Graham's inappropriate actions of groping her. Instead, he focused solely on Maggie's outburst, casting her as the sole perpetrator of unruly behaviour.

In a display of blatant injustice, Mr Spencer labelled Maggie as an "out of control thug," conveniently dismissing the underlying issue of Graham's misconduct. To him, Maggie's supposed lack of discipline at home was the root cause, emphasising that her broken family structure, absent father, and her mother's employment were to blame for her behaviour. The Headmaster callously insinuated that her actions were a predictable consequence of her upbringing, implying that she was destined for trouble.

The mention of her absent parents struck a deep nerve within Maggie. It was a low blow hitting her where it hurt the most. The pain of not having a traditional family setup weighed heavily on her, and Mr Spencer's insensitivity pushed her over the edge. Her true character emerged at that moment, and she retaliated with a fire fuelled by pent-up frustration and hurt.

Maggie's actions were instinctual, driven by a desperate need to defend herself and her family. Her emotional turmoil reached a boiling point, and she lashed out, unable to listen to the degradation any longer.

As she grappled with the aftermath of her outburst, she knew the repercussions imposed by the school of a suspension would bring forth more trouble for her family. She would have to carry the burden of ruining everything again. She was unsure what to do as she walked home but would have to deal with the consequences of her family's disappointment in her and thought they would be better off without her.

Maggie had decided to keep what had happened from her mother; she had her own key, and each day, Maggie would set off to school as usual and then hide until her mother went to work and then double back and let herself back into the house. Every time the postman walked up the path, Maggie held her breath, waiting for the letter explaining her suspension from school.

Within the week the letter arrived, Maggie steamed it open over the kettle in case she needed to reseal it. It was very official and stated that her mother must attend a meeting to discuss Maggie's suspension before they would consider reinstating her. They added that failure to participate in a discussion by one of Maggie's parents would result in her being removed from the school roll.

Maggie was shocked it was all so formal and decided to continue hiding out in the house until she was forced by circumstances to do something else. When she heard of her mother's plans to remarry, which meant leaving Salendine Nook, Maggie couldn't have been happier; it was the answer to her prayers. Elizabeth was shocked at Maggie's reaction to the news; she had expected all sorts of problems with Maggie, so she couldn't understand it when Maggie seemed overjoyed that she would have to go to a new school and leave all her friends.

ALL HAIL DOUGIE

As Dougie was led away for questioning, the prisoners on the block cheered and regaled him, he had dared to do what many others had wanted to do, but until Dougie came along, no one dared. The word soon got out that Dougie had taken Kieran down single-handed, and it was then speculated that he had done Chester too. When they thought back to the day Chester was murdered in the Church, they had all assumed that Dougie had been with Patrick. Still, no one had seen him until he bumped into them on his way to the toilets. Even the Governor wondered about this, especially after Patrick's shrewd story to rid the wing of Kieran Delaney, Patrick's possible rival. The word on the landing was that Patrick was the brains, and Chester was the muscle, a lethal combination.

Patrick had been taken from Kieran's cell to the hospital, where his stab wounds could be examined and dressed. Patrick was relieved to be alive and had mixed feelings at the news that Dougie had almost killed Kieran to protect him. He soon heard the rumours that he and Dougie would take over from Kieran, but that was not Patrick's intention. Patrick had heard from his solicitor that a new trial date had been set and wanted to give it one hundred per cent of his focus. This was possibly the last chance he had of being released before he was a very old man, and any slip-ups like the murder of an associate would not go well in his favour.

Kieran had been rushed to Wakefield Hospital as his condition was too critical to be dealt with in the prison hospital, and

SHELAGH TAYLOR

Patrick was grateful they would not be in the same ward.

Patrick had been stitched up and bound in bandages. He was told he needed to remain in hospital under observation for the next few days at least. His stab wounds had come close to puncturing his lungs and intestines, and it was still uncertain as to the full extent of the internal damage. Patrick was exhausted, cold and extremely worried; he fell into a fitful sleep.

He dreamt of trying to swim out of the prison gates on a river of blood, but he kept getting dragged back by a turning tide. In his dream, Patrick was trying to swim harder and harder against the current to get to the safety of the other side of the gates. But then he saw a rat swimming towards him with Chester's head in its enormous mouth. Chester's head was screaming and shaking in the rat's mouth, but it would not let go. Patrick could feel his heart banging against his chest, hear sirens, and see lights flashing in his eyes; he had never been so frightened and out of control. He fought with all his might to avoid the oncoming rat; Chester's eyes stared at him threateningly, coming closer and closer. Then he spotted the coal minor he had thrown down the pit shaft all those years ago and his father, almost a skeleton, also trying to reach him. Their skin hung off their bones, and both had gaping mouths with huge teeth, glistening and snapping open and shut. Patrick began screaming, unable to stop himself from careering towards them. He felt hands grab his arms and shouts of alarm, and then... nothing.

When he awoke, he was fixed up to a drip at the side of the bed, a nurse was checking his vital signs, and when he looked up at her and gasped, she said, "Oh, you are back with us again, are you, Patrick? We thought we had lost you for good a few hours back?"

Apparently, he had suffered a nonepileptic seizure due to the sudden change in the blood supply to his brain. It had been touch and go, but luckily he had pulled through. This event had extended Patrick's stay in the hospital, and the rest and time

THE PRICE OF SIMPLICITY

alone were what he needed to prepare his thoughts for a meeting with his barrister later that week. It would now take place in the hospital ward, which suited Patrick as fewer prisoners were listening in as he was currently the only prisoner in the room.

The following week he had a surprise visit from the Governor to commiserate with Patrick for his injuries; he expressed the sentiments that if the wheels had turned a little quicker, Kieran would have been moved before this unfortunate incident had occurred. He told Patrick that Dougie had admitted attacking Kieran to protect Patrick, his one true friend and that it had not been premeditated. The interview process took a long time to ascertain all the facts due to Dougie's speech impediment and processing speed. But the Governor said he was satisfied that neither Patrick nor Dougie had intended to harm Kieran before the incident. Dougie had not acted with murderous intent but reckless intent in defence of Patrick. Patrick had not retaliated as he had been unable to.

The Governor added that because Kieran had lived, wounding was the only charge made against Dougie. Still, if he died before the prosecution service had delivered on the case, then charges of manslaughter were guaranteed. The jury could very well find Dougie innocent depending on how good his solicitor was, but even if he was found guilty, it was a maximum of an additional five years on his life sentence, but that was unlikely.

Dougie had been allowed back on the wing and was greeted like a hero, Joe, his London friend, was the first by his side. Dougie had requested a hospital visit to see Patrick, which had been granted once Patrick was out of danger from his internal bleeding.

When Dougie saw Patrick wired up to drips and machines, he became agitated, fearing the worst, but when Patrick looked at him and smiled, Dougie calmed down and shuffled across the room to hold Patrick's hand. It was strange to see such a big ungainly man acting so genteel and benevolent to another man without any hint of sexual attraction. It was more like a father and son or brothers, and as the guard looked on, he was envious of such a close bond, closer than he had with his own flesh and blood.

Patrick thanked Dougie for saving his life but indicated that they would speak later by touching his ears to let Dougie know the guard was listening. Dougie nodded, understanding the nuance, and smiled. Patrick made small talk and was careful not to ask questions that would strain Dougie to answer with ease. For most of what Patrick said, Dougie could nod or shake his head, aware of the inferences in what had been asked or relayed. Patrick soon tired, and Dougie was taken back to the wing, assured of Patrick's recovery.

Joe had taken Dougie under his wing while waiting for Patrick's return; several London faces were interested in having Dougie as part of their firm but wanted to avoid stepping on Patrick's toes if he intended to take over from Kieran. Everyone was aware of Dougie's loyalty and the potential danger if they acted too hastily, but wanted it to be known that they were friends, not foes, if push came to shove. Patrick was due back in a couple of days, and even the most impatient prisoner could wait that long for what was going to be an essential change in dynamics.

Patrick's visit with his legal team brought the good news that left him optimistic about the re-trial. With Jack and his father long gone, people were more willing to come forward, but they were still very wary of Bill Black. But with Joe's evidence, that problem would be eliminated, and he could tie everything together, which the other witnesses against Jack were unaware of. As the evidence was new and compelling, the Court of Appeal granted the re-trial for January of Nineteen Seventy-One; Patrick had served just four years.

THE PLEASURE
AND THE PAIN

When Elizabeth told Maggie and Lizzie that she and Richard would get married in March, only six weeks away, they took the news much better than expected. Maggie had a good reason for this and lived each day on a knife's edge, waiting to be found out. Since her school suspension, Maggie had watched for the postman each day to intercept any letters. The first letter from the school had asked for a parental response. As it was not responded to, Maggie had expected another.

Maggie was tasked almost daily to steaming open any letters that fell through the letterbox. Most were Electricity or Gas bills, but Maggie only knew that once she opened and read them. Then the relief would wash over her, and Maggie would do her best to reseal them. Maggie had to admit most of the ones she steamed open and resealed looked like they had been mismanaged. Most were ripped or wrinkled, and her mother was getting suspicious, which jangled Maggie's nerves even more. Elizabeth had said she was going to speak to the postman when he called at the weekend and ask for an explanation of the condition of her post. Elizabeth suspected someone was opening and resealing the letters looking for money or a cheque, and she couldn't afford to lose any money sent to her. She had said, "Just suppose we win on the Premium Bonds, and somebody steals our money. I am not putting up with it any longer."

SHELAGH TAYLOR

It was another six weeks before her mother married, and they moved away; she couldn't get the letters that arrived on a Saturday and felt at a loss for the way forward. Maggie felt sick to her stomach. What could she do now?

By a stroke of luck, there were no letters on Saturday, and Maggie sighed in relief when she saw the postman walk down the road passing their house. She had decided that in the future, she would only open letters with envelopes that looked like the other school letter and leave the brown ones alone. They had fewer white ones, and instead of resealing any Maggie opened, she would burn them on the fire before her mother got home. Maggie relaxed now that she had a plan and spent the day in the garden, trying to avoid being seen by anyone from school. It was boring, not playing out, and Maggie felt like she wanted to do something exciting; she had been stuck inside the house all day for almost a week, driving her mad. Maggie was also a little afraid of seeing Graham, thinking he might get her back for punching him or try and grab her again and not stop.

Maggie decided she would explore places she had never been to before and, without telling anyone, set off out of the gate, turned right down Baker Street and walked until she got to Acre Street. She crossed the busy road that led onto the hospital, walked down Thornhill Avenue, and intended to continue until she reached Greenhead Park. Maggie was enjoying the freedom of being outside and exploring. She began singing to herself and making stories up in her head. Although Maggie had noticed somebody walking behind, she had yet to pay him much attention. But, the stretch of road ahead of her seemed dark and overhung with branches. Then, she realised there was no one else about, no houses, and the road ahead suddenly became long and intimidating. Maggie began looking around desperately for somewhere to run to if she needed to make an escape. Her heart was beating fast, and her breath became shorter and quicker.

THE PRICE OF SIMPLICITY

Maggie started to realise she had made a mistake not telling anyone where she was going, she could be anywhere, and no one would begin to miss her for hours yet. The sky seemed to be darkening by the second, and this spurred her on to run; she gave it everything she had, sprinting down the road, leaping over fallen branches. Maggie thought she could hear him starting to run, too, and she gulped. She could not reach the road before he caught up with her. She whispered and, panting, said, "Oh God, please help me, please help me."

Then she tripped; she appeared to run in mid-air, trying to catch her balance; she landed heavily on one knee, and pain screamed out of her impounded nerve endings. She struggled to her feet, staggering towards the light of the road ahead and what she hoped would be safety. Snivelling and snuffling, Maggie realised this might be the end of her causing her family any more torment, no more adventures; she didn't want to die; she had to keep trying even though she knew it was over. What would her mum say when she learned everything she had done in the past week. Would she be heartbroken to lose her, or would she be relieved that the Bane of her life, the poison that ruined everything for everyone, had finally gone?

Maggie was a fighter and would not be beaten by a bloody knee; she struggled to stand and then ran again. She decided if and when he got her, she would bite him as hard as she could. Maggie would keep biting down and biting as hard as she could while still having breath left in her body. She would bite and scratch and rake his skin under her nails. She had seen it on TV, where a murderer had claw marks on his face from his victim, which is how she would be remembered.

Then, he caught hold of her arm as she almost collapsed. Maggie's legs gave way, and she was on the ground, looking up helplessly into the face of a stranger with a black beard and dark eyes. He, too, was sweating and gasping for air; he held out his hand towards her, and Maggie sidled backwards with her back against the wall, almost lying down. She held her hands up and over her face with a look of terror as he spoke in a jiggered voice.

"I could hardly catch you. You dropped your gloves way back there." He turned and pointed up the road. He threw them at her as she stared up at him, and he carried on.

Maggie lay gasping for several moments before she pulled herself together and hurried towards the main road. She chastised herself for being stupid and wept tears of self-pity for almost being murdered, all alone with nobody knowing. Puffing out air that now steamed with the cold, Maggie began her return home. As she made the return journey, she stuck to the main road, but now she was worried that if her dad went past in his car and saw her on her own so far away from home, he would go berserk with her. Maggie quickened her pace and prayed he was elsewhere in Huddersfield and wouldn't see her.

Elizabeth was in a world of her own; her appointment had been made for Monday after work, which she thought would be ideal as it would all be ok by the time, she met Richard on a Saturday night. He would be surprised when she told him he didn't need to use a condom anymore. Elizabeth jostled her shoulders and smiled at the thought of it, but underneath, Elizabeth was nervous; she had heard it could hurt quite a bit. She was glad he had gone away to visit his father that weekend. It would give her a chance to think about the wedding and what she would take with her when she left to go and live with Richard.

Maggie walked in, shattering her peace; she looked upset but went straight upstairs so Elizabeth didn't get a chance to question her. Lizzie came home five minutes later, and Elizabeth started to light the fire. She had sat in the cold all day with a blanket around her, but now even the weak sunshine the day had brought disappeared; she suddenly felt freezing and shivering. Elizabeth swept the ashes from the night before and took them

THE PRICE OF SIMPLICITY

down to the cinders, a short distance from the house. On her return, she lit the fire and started making one of the children's favourites, which compiled of an onion boiled in the frying pan with salt and pepper, then sliced cheese and milk added until the cheese melted. The children loved the meal and would soak bread in the juice, licking their lips in pleasure.

When they sat down to eat, Elizabeth told the children to go to their Nanna's after school on Monday as she had an appointment in town and might be late. Maggie groaned and asked if she could just come home as usual? "No, Maggie, like I have said, I might be late, and I don't want you alone in the house for a long time; anything could happen."

Maggie replied, "I stay on my own on holidays, so what's the difference. Anyway, where are you going? Can't I come with you?"

Elizabeth replied, "No, you can't come with me. I am going to the Family Planning Clinic, and it is private. And, in the holidays, I am still just at the top of the road at work, and you know where I am; on Monday, you won't know where I am. That is the difference."

"What's a Family Planning Clinic?" both girls chorused.

Elizabeth just sighed and ignored them; she had enough on her plate at the moment without having to explain the facts of life to her daughters.

SISTER'S UNITED

Lizzie enjoyed seeing anyone suffer, unaware that life was not a game but could have a significant lifelong impact on others. When Lizzie had told her Nanna about her mother's wedding to Richard, she had hit the roof, making brutal, scathing remarks that went over Lizzie's head but comments she enjoyed hearing, knowing she had caused trouble. Lizzie smiled, knowing her family would be at each other's throats, giving Lizzie the satisfaction that others got from a united family front. She would store up these times to use against others later, adding her own venom. No matter how much others demonstrated love and sacrifice towards Lizzie, her feelings were shallow and unaffected by emotion. She was narcissistic and focused only on her own pleasure or suffering. Everyone else was incidental and of no importance.

On the surface, Lizzie exhibited as a sweet, shy, innocent girl, but beneath this façade hid a narcissistic child who exhibited traits of a complex and troubling personality disorder developed from the emotional neglect experienced early in life. Lizzie had an inflated sense of self-importance, a need for admiration, and a lack of empathy for others.

Even though Maggie had protected Lizzie from being a baby and at times made desperate scarifies to put Lizzie first, when Lizzie no longer needed Maggie's protection, she ceased to regard her feelings and well-being. Instead, she took satisfaction from exerting power and witnessing the turmoil she created within her family. No one had realised that Lizzie displayed a range of manipulative behaviours, seeking to exploit and control those around her for her own benefit.

Lizzie also had another secret she couldn't wait to expose to the family. Lizzie had learned today that Maggie had been suspended from school for punching a boy on the nose in front of the Headmaster. Now she was planning when she could break the news to create the most significant impact. She seemed to thrive on the chaos she created, finding a distorted sense of pleasure and validation in the pain and suffering of others, including her own family members.

Vera, Nanna, and Mum would no doubt spark off each other in their derision of Maggie. Yet another witness for Maggie's downfall would be even better. When Nanna suggested she would have to seek the help and advice of her sister Vera over the up-and-coming wedding, Lizzie thought that might be the perfect time to share her other news. Lizzie rubbed her hands together. She couldn't wait to innocently slip it into an already volatile situation.

When Vera met with Margaret on Saturday afternoon for tea and cakes, Margaret told of the news. Margaret said she hadn't seen Elizabeth speak to her since the fallout with her new boyfriend. When Elizabeth collected Lizzie on her way home from work, Margaret would send Lizzie along the passage, and Elizabeth would collect her on her way past. Margaret said when Lizzie had let the news of a wedding slip innocently out, Margaret had been so angry she knew then was not the time to confront Elizabeth. Margaret needed time to process the information Elizabeth was keeping secret. She wanted Vera's advice and maybe her presence when Elizabeth was confronted. Margaret was worried sick that Richard, Elizabeth's intended, would not be the man to raise her grandchildren in a safe environment. The night of the argument, he had spoken of living in Australia; if that was their plan, it would mean she would never see her grandchildren again, which was too much to bear for any woman.

Even though Vera had no room to discuss inappropriate relationships, she did. When she and Margaret sat down to tea for two at the British Home Stores café on Saturday afternoon, there was no stopping them. Vera talked at length about Elizabeth's poor choices to date and the aftermath of each of them. They had only ever seen Richard once, so they had little to go on. Margaret had found out from Lizzie that he had three children, all close in age, so he was obviously an animal who couldn't do without sex. They didn't know why he had custody of the children but guessed it must be an unsavoury reason. Lizzie had seen him less than a handful of times but could tell her Nanna that her mother had been to a 'Planning place'; that was also a secret. Vera and Margaret had surmised that this must be the 'Family Planning Clinic', so Elizabeth was already having sex with him. Vera said how disgusted she was that Elizabeth couldn't even wait until she was married. When Margaret took offence and suggested that Vera had been having sex with a married man, the only difference was he was married to someone else. Vera pursed her lips and frowned.

Talk all they wanted, the pair realised Elizabeth was a grown woman, and they could do little to stop her from taking her children where she pleased unless... Margaret had an idea circulating in her brain, but not yet ready to be a plan. Vera asked, "Unless what?"

"Just give me a minute Vera." As she thought, Margaret put her thumb up the side of her mouth and the rest of her hand on her chin. "I've got it; all we need to do is tell Danny about the marriage. He will never let Elizabeth take those children away. He loves them too much."

Margaret had an idea where he lived but had also seen him at the bingo hall she was a member of on a Saturday night. "If I don't get a chance to talk with him tonight, I will tell him we need

THE PRICE OF SIMPLICITY

to see him, and he will call on Sunday when he has dropped the children back off at Elizabeth's house."

Happy with the plan, they returned to Margaret's house so that Vera could join her at the bingo that night and, if necessary, be there when Danny called in the following day. This was a significant problem, and they didn't want to waste any opportunities to scupper Elizabeth's plans to secretly marry and whisk the children away.

Although they saw Danny at bingo, the meeting was brief; Margaret explained that she needed him to call at her house after he had dropped the children back home the following day. This immediately made Danny think that the news was grave and about his children. Still, Margaret calmed him by telling him it was about a romance Elizabeth was involved in and thought he should know about. She had something of magnitude to say to him. Placated but a little despondent, Danny left them to return to his wife, agreeing to call around four in the afternoon.

When Danny heard the news the next day, it wasn't until they mentioned the possibility of Elizabeth taking the children to Australia that he started to panic and let his emotions get the better. He said he wanted to see Elizabeth immediately; he would not leave it another day, as no one knew when she may marry and leave. Lizzie had mentioned she would leave her school soon but was unsure when. Margaret and Vera said they would go too, and the three of them got into Danny's car and sped the three hundred yards to Elizabeth's house.

When Elizabeth saw the three of them walking along the path towards the house, she could not imagine what they wanted but knew it must be meaningful; she only hoped it would not be bad news.

When Danny knocked, Lizzie ran to answer it and was amazed at the sight of her Nanna, Dad and Aunty Vera, all looking angry.

193

Margaret didn't wait to be asked in. She brushed past Lizzie and immediately told Elizabeth they needed some answers. They were not leaving until they were satisfied that Maggie and Lizzie were safe. Maggie stared at them, as did Lizzie, but where Maggie had no idea why they were there, Lizzie knew full well. She would not waste this opportunity to spill the beans about Maggie's suspension. When Elizabeth asked them what they meant, wondering if they had found out about the wedding, Lizzie said, "Is it because Maggie has had to leave Salendine Nook?"

Everyone looked at her, and she cast her eyes down as if she was upset; Maggie's mouth dropped open, and her eyes looked like saucers. They cast their eyes towards Maggie and then back to Elizabeth, who was looking bewildered. "Maggie hasn't had to leave Salendine Nook, Lizzie. But, I told you that when Richard and I marry, you will leave your schools and go to a new school near Richard's house."

She could have killed Lizzie for telling them and knew they were here to cause trouble. But, Lizzie stuttered, "No, Maggie has already had to leave her school; a boy at my school told me that Maggie has been kicked out of Salendine Nook for punching a boy in the nose, and the Headmaster saw her do it. Didn't you, Maggie?"

Elizabeth turned towards Maggie in disbelief, "Is this true, Maggie? Why did you punch someone?"

Maggie pulled her mouth wide into a grimace, knowing she had been found out and was now in deep trouble. "Because he tried to rape me!"

Danny, Elizabeth, Margaret and Vera chorused at once, "He what!"

Sobbing, Maggie now continued, "He tried to rape me, he kept

THE PRICE OF SIMPLICITY

doing it, and I wanted him to stop, but he wouldn't, and when he grabbed me in class, we were sent to see Mr Spencer; he tried again, and I punched him. I didn't know how else to stop him raping me."

The wedding was forgotten as they gathered around Maggie, asking her questions, trying to console her and Danny, angrier than she could remember ever seeing him, demanding to know, "Who the FUCKING RAPIST WAS THAT TOUCHED MY MAGGIE?"

Maggie told them Graham's name but didn't tell them where he lived. When asked if the school knew she had been raped by Graham, she said that she thought they knew but had said that because her dad didn't live with them and her mother worked, it was to be expected.

Now all of them were fired up; Margaret said she was going to the police, Danny was going to kill the 'Fucking Headmaster and Graham, Elizabeth was standing trying to hug Maggie and repeating, "Oh my God, why didn't you tell me, Maggie. What have you been doing since it happened? I thought you were a lot quieter than usual. I knew something was the matter. Oh, Maggie, if only you had told me."

Vera chipped in, "I suppose YOU were too loved up to even notice your child in agony?"

Everyone had momentarily forgotten about the wedding, but that would have to wait. This was far more important.

Elizabeth turned on Vera and told her to hold her vicious tongue. Then a row erupted until Maggie shouted to everyone, "PLEASE JUST BE QUIET AND STOP ARGUING."

The arguing stopped abruptly, and things settled down. Plans were made to sort it all out on Monday, Elizabeth would take the day off work, Margaret would go with her to school, and Vera could look after Maggie. "I don't need looking after; I'm twelve."

"You have had a shock, Maggie, and we want to take care of you. Danny, you wouldn't be able to keep your temper if you went to the school, so I suggest you call back tomorrow after you finish work around 4:30-5pm." Margaret coped best when she was organising, and everyone seemed happy to follow her instructions.

Danny reluctantly agreed and took Maggie in his arms; she would always be the little girl he had lived with before poor Bernadette had her accident. For him, those times were so frozen in his heart that neither Maggie nor Lizzie would ever grow up in his eyes. It was too hard to bear if he thought he had moved on.

Everyone left, leaving Elizabeth, Maggie and Lizzie to cope alone. Elizabeth kept looking at Maggie until Maggie couldn't stand it any longer and went upstairs to read a book. She was afraid of what the school would say, she was ashamed her dad had heard about the rape, and she felt empty inside. She wished she could magic it all away, but she couldn't, and she would just have to face it all again tomorrow when they came back, and all started talking about it again.

This hadn't gone as Lizzie had intended, but it was still a show to be proud of.

The next morning Lizzie was sent off to school and was seething she would miss the fun. Margaret and Vera arrived with chocolate and a comic for Maggie; Elizabeth looked ashen as if she hadn't slept a wink, which she hadn't.

When Elizabeth and Margaret had gone, Vera sat down with Maggie and asked her to tell her exactly how he raped her. Everyone else had avoided the question, but Vera had less of a filter. When Maggie explained that Graham had grabbed her

THE PRICE OF SIMPLICITY

many times, he had looked inside her knickers and tried to pull her vest up. When Vera said and then what happened, Maggie said, "I usually fought him off, but he was getting stronger, and so I punched him."

Vera added, "But when did he rape you?"

Maggie replied, "That is rape, Vera, that is what my dad did to my mum, and you all said he tried to rape her?"

It dawned on Vera then that Maggie had not been a victim of rape but had been subjected to an over-amorous boy groping her. She cracked out laughing, partly due to nerves about what she was frightened to hear and partly due to the fact that Elizabeth and Margaret were at the school accusing a boy of rape and the Headmaster of doing nothing. There was no way of letting them know what she had found out, and they couldn't do anything until they got back home. Maggie stared at her when Vera laughed, and she explained the difference between being groped and raped without too much detail. Maggie asked if they would be cross with her for getting it wrong, but Vera reassured her that she would stick up for her; it was their fault really for letting her hear such things in the first place. "They will be more relieved than cross Maggie, so don't worry, love."

When they returned from the school, they said they had made a complaint, and the Headmaster had been very apologetic. They told the Headmaster they would involve the police and the newspaper if nothing was done. Mr Spencer said he would speak to Graham and any witnesses to the incident that day, and they would lift the suspension. He had begged them not to take the matter to the police until everyone had been interviewed and that he would have Graham's parents brought in to be part of the school investigation, something he should have done immediately.

When they left, Elizabeth and Margaret felt they had been

SHELAGH TAYLOR

listened to and that the school was taking the accusation seriously and admitted fault. The Headmaster said he had been so shocked to witness Maggie punching the boy that he had gone off the rails and knew he shouldn't have. Again he apologised, knowing he would lose his job if this all came out.

Arriving home, they could hear Vera and Maggie laughing as they approached the door and looked at each other, puzzled. When they went inside, Vera and Maggie were playing a game of cards that Maggie kept catching Vera cheating at, making them laugh. The tension in the house had gone. Vera said, "Before you say anything more, you had better sit down; we have something we need to say."

When everything was explained, the relief was audible. Elizabeth said they would have to go back and tell Mr Spencer; Margaret said, "Let him stew; he deserves it after what he said and you and Danny, Elizabeth."

Danny was never so relieved and hugged Maggie so tightly she had to fight for breath. He leant over to Elizabeth and, in front of Margaret and Vera, wished her luck with her wedding and said, "This Richard guy is a lucky man Elizabeth, but he will be a dead man if ever he lays a finger on my children."

Elizabeth smiled and thanked Danny and said she had no intention of moving to Australia; the furthest she was going was a little village called Marsden on the way to Oldham.

Elizabeth decided that she would wait for the official letter from Salendine Nook dismissing Maggie's suspension from school and the outcome of the meeting with Graham's parents before sending Maggie back to school. Vera had said that Maggie could go and stay with her in Meltham for a few days, and that would keep her out of the way for a while. Elizabeth was conscious that Graham's parents would be hearing all about his part in the fracas and hoped they would stop his unwanted sexual advances

THE PRICE OF SIMPLICITY

towards any girl in the future. He was lucky that Danny hadn't been the one to catch him, as he would have strung the boy up if he had.

Vera would be glad of the company, and she knew that Margaret would be jealous that she had Maggie and not her. But Margaret worked and lived in the same area as the school, so it made sense for Maggie to go to Meltham. Hopefully, Maggie would stay out of trouble whilst she was there.

Danny had called first thing Monday morning and was satisfied with the plans; he said he would take Vera and Maggie to Meltham in his Kirklees work van. It was against the rules to carry passengers, but abiding by the rules was never a strong suit for Danny. Danny took Elizabeth and Maggie up to Margaret's to collect Vera. Maggie squashed into the passenger seat and waved goodbye to Elizabeth and Margaret. Lizzie had reluctantly gone to school peeved that she was no longer the centre of attention, and her plans to make Maggie look bad had failed despite the ensuing drama.

THE ACQUITTAL

As he departed for the hearing, the Governor bid Patrick farewell, expressing his genuine hope that they would never cross paths again as inmates and warden. However, he told Patrick; if he followed his dreams and dedication to working with prisoners who had endured severe childhood abuse, he would be welcome in prison anytime. The Governor appreciated Patrick's wisdom and cooperation, recognising the potential positive impact Patrick could have. He also emphasised the importance of staying connected with Dougie, who had earned a reputation for himself with Patrick's guidance.

Evidence had been heard from Jack's gambling club employees at the time of the kidnapping. Each testified that although they had not seen the girl brought onto the premises, they had witnessed him taking food and water to the room where she was kept for as far as they knew 4-5 days.

One of the witnesses had been working the night the foreign-looking gentleman had been taken up the stairs to the room and heard the girl screaming. They also testified that Jack had removed the man bringing him back into the club. They added that although Jack was annoyed with the man, he did not have him removed from the club. All the witnesses confirmed Jack had a bad drug problem. He would hallucinate, causing injuries to those people who offended him in any way. Jack's accountant confirmed that Jack and the club were in a great deal of debt and that Jack had promised when a major deal that he was working on with some associates from London was complete

THE PRICE OF SIMPLICITY

in a few days, then his debts would be cleared. He would leave Huddersfield, abandoning his wife and child too for good.

One of the prostitutes who had worked with Ruby, who had not come forward for the original trial due to fear and intimidation, swore she had witnessed Jack drowning Ruby in the canal under the viaduct where she worked.

With permission from his boss in London, Joe could offer overwhelming evidence against Bill Black. This man had betrayed one of the London associates Joe was affiliated with, and Joe's evidence was payback.

Then one by one, people that had known Patrick's true intention of freeing Rosie from the club, even if it had meant him losing his life, came forward to give evidence in favour of Patrick. Again their reasoning was fear of Bill Black and others involved at the time. Most spoke of how Patrick and Cameron Murphy had worked tirelessly and put themselves at significant risk to free Rosie. Cameron Murphy, a local doctor who had been a frequent visitor to the club and had been stripped of his licence due to alcoholism, still had a sense of justice and protection over the innocent. When Cameron Murphy had heard about the kidnapping and remembered it had been him that brought Rosie into this world, he had become resolute in his efforts to save her.

Rosie attended the hearing and was once again called as a witness; after all these years, she still wasn't sure if Jack had been a friend or foe. Still, she had heard he was her father before he got killed and wanted him to be innocent and to have fought to save her so profoundly that she painted that picture in her head. Now, Rosie was not sure of anything. She understood that he had shown the man into the room she was kept in, and he did have a key to give her food for all those days, so she surmised that he could have if he had wanted also release her. Hearing that he may have also murdered her mother saddened her beyond belief. To have lost a mother who doted on her, gave her everything that she never had, would have died for her if necessary, was more distressing than she could imagine.

Marilyn had been in court too, listening with a heavy heart to the hurt in all the lives involved, including Jack, who had been a decent man in his youth and, if it hadn't been for the drugs, would have been horrified by his actions. As Marilyn looked intently at Patrick, the ravages of time were evident on his once very handsome face, and the vivid scars had shocked her too. His body was not what it once was, but looking down, Marilyn realised neither was hers. Life can be so cruel sometimes.

After the acquittal hearing, where Patrick was given a dismissal of all charges related to the crime for which he was initially convicted by the court, he was released.

When Rosie left the stand, she met up with Marilyn in the foyer, and they hugged and wept together until Patrick walked out of court a free man. Rosie walked up to him and held out her hand, begging his forgiveness for not trusting him so long ago and incidentally causing him to serve a prison sentence. Rosie remarked that if only she could turn back the clock, she would see things through different eyes. He just replied, "Amen to that. If any of us had the power to turn back the clock, we would all do things very differently in one way or another. Perhaps it was all meant to be for a bigger, more profound reason we are all unaware of. I am glad you have found your way in life and have a career that you excel at."

Patrick winked at Marilyn, and she blushed as she always had. Then she said, "Are you still in touch with Elizabeth Ryan, Patrick?"

Patrick lifted his head at the mention of Elizabeth's name; his eyes showed only sorrow and pain. "I haven't seen Elizabeth for the past four years, but I would like to let her know of today's outcome and hope she can find it in her heart to forgive me,"

THE PRICE OF SIMPLICITY

Patrick asked if she knew her whereabouts.

Marilyn said the last time she had seen her was when she collected Danny's money from the court a few months ago. She looked happy enough and had just started attending a single's club in Huddersfield, but I haven't seen or heard from her since.

Patrick brightened at this news, realising that Elizabeth must still be single and perhaps would listen to him now he had been exonerated of her uncle's murder?

Patrick left Wakefield County Court and headed towards the railway station. He hoped to get the next train to Huddersfield.

SOMEBODY IS WATCHING

Patrick arrived in Huddersfield on Friday afternoon, determined to take time and not to arrive late at night as he had done in the past. He found a modest B&B on Trinity Street, just a short walk from the station. Patrick decided to get a good night's sleep and clean up properly before arriving on Elizabeth's doorstep. He yearned for the simple pleasures of a private bath and leisurely shave, free from prison life's rigid schedules and routines. He may even bring Elizabeth some flowers, a small gesture to express his affection.

Saturday morning arrived, and Patrick awoke feeling remarkably refreshed after enjoying the most peaceful sleep he had experienced in the past four years. He felt rejuvenated and eager to reunite with Elizabeth once again.

After washing up, Patrick headed down to the breakfast area of the B&B. As he savoured his first meal since gaining his freedom, he couldn't help but anticipate the meeting, his nerves gradually intensifying. It was only nine in the morning, and Patrick wanted to arrive when Elizabeth had also had time to freshen herself. Patrick wanted everything to be perfect, just like he had imagined over and over, lying on his bunk in his prison cell.

Walking along the road towards Baker Street, Patrick's pace slowed, his heart pounding with excitement and anxiety. He couldn't help but daydream about the moment he would lay eyes

THE PRICE OF SIMPLICITY

on Elizabeth again. In his daydream, he pictured her opening the door, her face lighting up as she threw her arms around his neck. He imagined the warmth of their embrace, the tender kisses shared, and the heartfelt words expressing his deep love for her. The anticipation filled him with joy and torment as the longing to be reunited with Elizabeth consumed his thoughts.

He felt butterflies inside as he approached the gate leading up to Elizabeth's house. He realised it had been a long time since he had seen Elizabeth. The door opened, and Patrick froze. Seeing a dishevelled man emerging from the house filled him with jealousy and anger. Clearly, this man had spent the night with Elizabeth, and Patrick's mind raced with thoughts of their intimate moments together. Patrick was transfixed as the man turned and kissed what must be Elizabeth stood out of sight behind the door. Patrick imagined her naked and glowing from her lovemaking, giddy with the afterglow of sex. Patrick brought his fists up to his eyes, placing his knuckles above his eyebrows, trying to halt the pain in his head.

Realising he was standing facing the gate, Patrick stepped back and out of sight, he had no idea what he would do, but as the man exited the gate, Patrick began to follow him. Every nerve in his body rankled to kill this man, to beat and maim him; he clenched and unclenched his fists, clenched his teeth together so hard his jaw ached as he filled with a pain that was hard to bear.

The man went to the bus stop and caught the next bus into the town centre, transferring to a trolley bus to a place called Marsden. Richard got on the bus and went upstairs; Patrick sat downstairs at the front to get off at the same time as the man without raising suspicion. Patrick still held the flowers and felt a little silly but thought they might be helpful as an excuse for his trip if Richard questioned him.

Patrick was shaken out of his reverie when he saw Richard appear at the front of the bus, ready to alight. At the last minute,

Patrick jumped up and got off after Richard, following him along the road.

Richard turned and headed up the path of a house with its curtains still closed; Patrick walked past, then when Richard was inside, he doubled back and stood looking at the home. Richard looked out on Patrick as the curtains opened downstairs, staring at the house. Patrick had no choice but to walk up the path and knock on the door. He could hear children crying, and Patrick guessed that the man must be married.

When Richard opened the door, Patrick held up the flowers and said he was looking for Glenda Smith, the first name that popped into his head. He could see three young children behind Richard and made a quip about having his hands full, adding, "Or is it the missus who has that job?"

Richard replied, "No, she buggered off a year ago; the kids are all mine now. I don't know any Glenda Smith, I know a Margaret Smith, but her husband wouldn't be very pleased with you bringing her flowers." Richard laughed at his own joke.

Patrick thanked him anyway and left; he walked on the road until he was out of sight of the house and then crossed the street to catch the return bus to Huddersfield. He still needed to figure out why he had followed the man or what good it had done. He was disturbed that the three children were most likely alone since the previous night, but Patrick had no proof.

When he reached Huddersfield, he retraced his steps to return to Elizabeth's house. Patrick knew now she was in a relationship and might not welcome him as she once had. He had written her a note while on the bus, as he had realised, it would be a shock seeing him after all this time. A message might better prepare Elizabeth for his arrival.

Standing again at Elizabeth's gate, he saw the door open, and a young girl, that must be Maggie judging by her apparent age, came skipping along the path. When she got to the gate, Patrick held out the flowers and the note and asked Maggie if she would deliver these to her mother before she went out. "Tell her it's her old friend Patrick and he would love to have the chance to talk to her."

Maggie shrugged, took the flowers and note, and ran back to the house; she raced inside shouting, "Mum, there's a man at the gate with loads of scars, and he has given me some flowers for you. He's still there; I think he is waiting?"

Elizabeth's eyes opened as wide as they would go; she began to tremble and hesitantly made her way to peek through the net curtains to the gate. When Elizabeth saw Patrick looking towards the house, she clasped her hand over her mouth as her mouth dropped open. Elizabeth jumped back in shock at the sight of Patrick.

"Who is it, Mum?" inquired Maggie, "What does he want?"

"His name is Father Heron; he knew us long ago, even before you were born. He used to come to our house and play with you and Bernadette; he was our priest. The memory of Patrick playing with Maggie and Bernadette filled Elizabeth's eyes with, tears spilling down her cheeks. The memory seemed so long ago, another lifetime, before…

THE PRICE OF SIMPLICITY

Elizabeth and Maggie jumped at the knock on the door; Lizzie had just been coming down the stairs and opened it, unaware of the conversation that had just occurred. She stared at the man on the doorstep, holding flowers, and shouted, "Mum."

Elizabeth brushed herself down and stepped towards the door; she didn't have time to plan, just act. Elizabeth's eyes lifted to look at the man before her and quietly said, "Patrick." Her hand reached up and briefly touched his new scars, the old ones so faded they were barely visible anymore. Realising what she was doing, Elizabeth quickly pulled her hand away as if she had been burnt. Maggie and Lizzie watched her every move, wondering who this man was and why he was there.

Patrick looked deep into Elizabeth's face, unable to stop; he had tears in his eyes that lingered too long on Elizabeth. Tilting his head slightly to take more of her in, Patrick regained his composure and said, "Well, if this one is Maggie, then this one must be Lizzie."

The girls smiled at his recognition, and he asked them how their daddy was keeping and made them laugh when he asked them if they had started work yet. Patrick winked at Elizabeth as he teased the girls, saying, "Surely, you must be teenagers by now. Maggie, you look sixteen, and Lizzie, you look almost as old. You can't still be at school?"

THE PRICE OF SIMPLICITY

Lizzie answered quick as a flash, "Well, she isn't. She got kicked out for fighting."

Elizabeth shouted, "LIZZIE, stop that talk, it was all a mistake, and you know it."

"But she did get suspended, didn't you, Maggie?"

Elizabeth quickly tried to change the subject by offering Patrick a cup of coffee, which he gratefully accepted. As Elizabeth made the coffee, Patrick entertained the girls, telling them funny stories about his time in Spain. Elizabeth was on pins knowing sooner or later, Maggie or Lizzie would ask about Patrick's scars, and just as she was walking over with two cups of hot coffee in her hands, it happened.

"Did you get those scars on your face in Spain?" asked Maggie.

Patrick was very calm when he replied, "No, Maggie, I didn't. You know how sometimes things happen that you have no control over, and the consequences are just a natural occurrence, a bit like your suspension. Well, something I didn't like happened to me too, which was the consequence of that. But you can't be a 'Super Hero' without a few scars, right?"

The girls laughed at Patrick's explanation, and the situation was defused. It was lovely to see how good Patrick was with the girls, patient, fun and on their level without talking down to them. It was apparent they liked him, and Elizabeth couldn't help but compare the relationship to Richard's one with them. Her eyes lingered again on Patrick, taking in the sight before her. Elizabeth longed to ask him questions, knowing he had been given a life sentence four years ago; how could he be a free man? The questions, though, would just have to wait; Elizabeth knew that anything discussed in front of Maggie or Lizzie could be repeated to her mother, Danny or Richard. Elizabeth needed

209

SHELAGH TAYLOR

to ensure that did not happen until she knew the full facts; for all she knew right now, he could be a fugitive on the run and wouldn't they all love that!

Elizabeth had hoped the girls would get bored and go out to play, but they were too perceptive for that. They knew something was happening, and neither wanted to miss it. Elizabeth was thankful that Friday was her day to see Richard; she could not imagine what she would say or do if he turned up whilst Patrick was here. She was worried her mother might call in on her way home from meeting Vera in town. Since they had put the argument behind them to stand united as a family should, things had returned to how it was with Margaret on call to support them all. Elizabeth had been grateful the unpleasantness was over; she understood why her mother disliked Richard; she knew her mother only wanted the best for her and the children and didn't want to see them hurt again. But, her mother would have to learn to accept him once they were married, and he hopefully proved Margaret wrong.

As the afternoon wore on with Patrick, it began to get dark; the winter chill had ascended as the sun sank. Elizabeth turned up the gas fire shivering, but it didn't seem to penetrate the biting air around them. Elizabeth was sat in her usual armchair, and the girls and Patrick were squashed up on the two-seater settee. Patrick asked if they could walk to fish and chip shops nearby, and he would treat them all. The girls excitedly said they could walk to one just down the road. Patrick offered to take them while Elizabeth buttered some bread. Patrick was aware that the day had been a shock, he knew she probably needed some breathing space, but he didn't want to leave without talking things over with her, which would have to be when the girls were in bed. Patrick only hoped Elizabeth was in the same frame of mind and would be okay with him staying until they were alone long enough to chat.

210

THE PRICE OF SIMPLICITY

As he rose from the couch, he caught Elizabeth looking at him and wished he knew the thoughts in her head. The girls ran, got their coats and shoes, and almost dragged Patrick out of the house to go and get the chip supper.

As soon as the door closed behind them, Elizabeth dropped onto the settee, exhaled deeply and shook her head in despair. She was worried about when and how this saga would end; the tension she had felt since Patrick's arrival had knotted her stomach until she was in agony. It wasn't that Elizabeth didn't want him here; Elizabeth was just so afraid of him being found in her house. She began to worry that he may not leave at the end of the evening; how would she explain her betrothal to Richard? Elizabeth felt she had somehow betrayed Patrick with Richard, but that wasn't the case. Waiting for Patrick to return also felt like she was betraying Richard; why was life so hard, with all these damn dilemmas?

Elizabeth, she still felt excited at the thought of Patrick's touch on her body, she had only just begun to experience sex again after many years of abstinence, and although it had felt good, Elizabeth didn't crave Richard's touch like she had Patrick's. Elizabeth thought if she could just sleep with Patrick once, then maybe she would realise he was no different from other men, that sex was, in fact, just sex and nothing more. But how could she be sure without trying it? Elizabeth thought how similar Eve must have felt when she first tempted Adam in the Garden of Eden; it was the wrapping, not the exciting goods. Even though Patrick had aged considerably and now sported even more scars, they added to his allure. Elizabeth realised for the first time today that she would not resist; she would take him as she had always imagined. The illusion was earth-shattering and so addictive she would risk everything just to be a part of the promised, forbidden pleasure.

The door banged open, and the children ran in ahead of Patrick,

211

who was aware that Elizabeth looked at him differently now. The evening appeared to slow down, and each movement that she made was exaggerated and sensual, making Patrick burn with desire for this woman who stood before him. Both adults are acutely aware of the electricity passing between them.

When the chips were eaten and the paper disposed of, the girls and Patrick sat back down on the settee; this time, Patrick took the seat nearest Elizabeth's chair and casually dropped his hand over the side in reach of her. Elizabeth looked for a long time at the muscular arm and the hand that waited for her to touch and finally succumbed. Elizabeth lazily dropped her hand over the edge of her chair, and their fingers met for the first time in four years.

Simultaneously, Patrick and Elizabeth closed their eyes, the impact of their touch too much to allow any other focus but their singleness. Their breath slowly froze to a halt as they gasped and held the air that had become so dense in their throats that it was impossible to take another breath. Each heart quickened to match the drumming that had begun to beat in Patrick and Elizabeth's heads. Elizabeth finally let go and dropped her head, exhausted by the emotional impact the touch had imparted upon her. Elizabeth knew she was destined to lie with Patrick as soon as they could organise the privacy they yearned for.

For years, the intense magnetism between Patrick and Elizabeth had simmered beneath the surface, an unspoken desire that had fuelled their every interaction. Fate had always conspired against them, pulling them apart just as they were on the brink of surrendering to their long-held yearning. Time ticked by, and the children relaxed in Patrick's company, watching a series of 'On the Buses' that Patrick had never seen before. However, Maggie and Lizzie began to fill him in on the characters, making him laugh out loud at their childish explanations.

THE PRICE OF SIMPLICITY

Innocently, Lizzie mentioned how much 'Stan Butler', the bus driver in 'On the Buses', looked like Mum's boyfriend, Richard. "Do you know Richard Patrick?"

Elizabeth had frozen, not daring to move her eyes away from the television to look at Patrick, but in a way, glad that Richard's name had been mentioned. Elizabeth knew she should have mentioned him before; she had the whole day to tell Patrick about her upcoming wedding but had chosen not to. Part of this was that Elizabeth felt guilty, but also, it was because she didn't want this feeling to end. She knew Patrick was very moral and may now stand up and leave without another word. The silence was audible before Patrick replied, "I don't think I have met him, but if he is your mother's friend, then I am sure I will like him."

When the program ended, Elizabeth told Maggie and Lizzie it was bedtime, followed by complaining and begging to stay up late. Elizabeth remained firm, saying she and Patrick had adult things to discuss, and she didn't want them to spoil such a nice day.

Reluctantly, the girls collected their hot water bottles and took them to bed, shouting, "Good night Patrick."

Patrick smiled at the simple pleasure he got from having two little girls wishing him good night and shouted his reply, "Sleep tight, and don't let the bed bugs bite."

Patrick's heart swelled, and he looked over at Elizabeth and smiled, adding, "I have done so many things in my life and yet, missed so much more. I wish I had been here for you since Bernadette's passing instead of running away from my feelings. I had a long time to think in the Spanish mountains and even more time in Wakefield Prison.

Patrick felt the need to explain his reasoning. He put Elizabeth's mind at rest that he was no longer a Priest and that lying with him would no longer be a sin.

My time as a priest is over; I have done too many things to consider myself in a personal relationship with God or the Catholic Church and its teachings. I have chosen a new vocation that I think will be more beneficial to others and a better way to serve God. My experience inside the prison has developed a unique insight into the failings of our systems when it comes to rehabilitating prisoners that have acted under duress, both physically and mentally. In other words, childhood abuse victims have no option but to learn to survive; we all have a breaking point, and when this happens, they are punished instead of rehabilitated.

But, now I am back, we can be together again, and life can be fulfilling for us all; we don't have to fight our feelings any longer, Elizabeth. You can explain to Richard that now I am back, you want to be with me and end things with him so he can move on."

Elizabeth turned to Patrick, "If only everything in life was so simple, but it isn't; everything comes at a price. I have told Richard I love him and accepted his marriage proposal; I can't just walk away from that. One person's happiness is another's misery, and if I accept you in my life, I have to hurt Richard, and I am not sure he deserves that. You have no idea how much you wounded me the last time you were here, Patrick. Yes, I have longed for you most of my adult life, but you have always turned your back on me. Richard has always embraced his feelings towards me, and I am now betrothed to him."

Patrick tried to reason with Elizabeth, "You say that you have told Richard you love him and accepted his proposal, but are you 'In Love with him?'"

Patrick took Elizabeth's hands in his and added. "Striving to please everybody is impossible, Elizabeth and I should know; I spent most of my life as a priest, always trying to do the right thing and avoid hurting anybody. But investing solely in one area may yield short-term gains, but it can come at the cost of long-term well-being and overall life satisfaction. When you talk of not wanting to hurt Richard, a man you have admitted loving but not deeply in love with, you surely understand that the short-term satisfaction of marrying him will not serve you or your children in the long term. You are as convenient to him as he is to you, and that is not love, Elizabeth. Elizabeth, I have lost too much to lose you again. You will be mine, and Richard can find another; I could never have anyone except you in my arms or bed."

His words touched Elizabeth, and their bodies gravitated towards one another; he enfolded her in his arms, their lips finally meeting in a passionate, long-awaited kiss. The pent-up desire and a culmination of years of longing finally met in this stolen moment. Elizabeth surrendered to the fiery chemistry that had always burned between her and Patrick.

He slowly undressed Elizabeth, gasping and breathing hard, as each layer of clothing was removed. She unbuttoned his shirt and opened it touching his body hungrily, but then pulled back as if on fire as she felt the risen scars of his recent stabbing and the beatings he had endured in his youth, revealing long-held secrets.

Now, too hungered by desire, her lips once again sought his, their touch both tender and urgent, exploring the contours of each other with an intimate familiarity they never thought they would experience.
Throughout their lovemaking, their connection was far more profound than a physical experience. They poured their suppressed emotions into every caress, every whispered word, and every shared breath. They were lost in the intoxicating pleasure, vulnerability, and a profound sense of fulfilment for

the moment.

Patrick was well aware his pleasure would not last if he took her now and wanted to prolong this moment as long as he could to ensure Elizabeth was satisfied before he was released from his sexual tension.

Elizabeth finally began to moan and arch her body, gripping Patrick with all her might and pulling him against her. Moving her body so that he had no choice but to take her. He thrust deep inside her body, his mouth open to allow his shortened breath to escape and held her so tight he thought she might break in two. Finally, and simultaneously they moaned together, kissing and pressing into each other, for any final moments of pleasure, before sinking down into the floor where they lay spent. Glowing with the sweat of their exertions and the love they had held for over a decade.

The air around their naked bodies grew colder as they lay in each other's arms. Still, neither wanted to break the spell of laying together for the first time, their bodies glistening with a sheen of sweat and their hearts finally at peace.

REALITY COMES KNOCKING

They lay together until the dawn broke. Elizabeth had brought a blanket down from her bed, and they snuggled up together, at peace with the world and the fantasy they had become embroiled in.

Elizabeth's eyes fluttered open, and the weight of guilt and realisation hit her like a fist, awakening her from the dream-like state she had allowed herself to sink into, thrusting reality into her face. Panic seized her, tightening its grip around her racing heart as she grappled with the turmoil threatening to consume her. What was she going to do now?

Her first thought was to get rid of Patrick before the children came downstairs. Elizabeth began to panic, unable to rationalise her thoughts. Fear tinging every decision, suffocating her ability to think clearly. She was betrothed to Richard and had promised to marry him in less than a month, and here she was, lying naked next to Patrick after a night of unbridled sex. Elizabeth was relieved that at least she had the coil to prevent pregnancy. What was she going to do? Elizabeth raised her clenched hands towards her mouth and looked at Patrick.

Patrick's face was serene, relaxed and almost angelic, even with the vivid scaring. Elizabeth shook his shoulder, and he blinked, trying hard to open his eyes, before turning towards Elizabeth and gently kissing her on the forehead. Startled by the stiffness of her body, he opened his eyes fully and looked down on Elizabeth, who sat up with a look of terror. "You must go, Patrick; you can't be here when the children wake up," Elizabeth spoke urgently as if she was about to cry.

"Calm down, Elizabeth, I know you need time to explain things to the children, and I don't want to cause you any anguish. But please don't be afraid. It is what we both want, and if you find it too hard to explain everything to Richard, I will happily either be with you or do it for you. You need never be afraid again now that I am by your side."

Elizabeth felt like screaming; she wished it was possible to just disappear and not have to face anything or anyone, it was all too much, and Patrick was acting like it was nothing. "I can't face any of this now, Patrick; I need time to process what happened before explaining anything to the children or Richard. And... I also have to consider my mother's feelings; as far as she knows, you are the man that murdered her brother. I am sorry, Patrick, but you must allow me some time."

The words began pouring out of Elizabeth as she questioned her morality. "We have not even spoken of how or why you were released, things have happened too quickly, and I never should have allowed it. The past should have stayed in the past, I was just starting to build a new life, and now I feel like I am again in torment. Last night was a dream, a wonderful, erotic, exciting dream. But my reality is dealing with the kids, my mother, Richard, and Danny. I am not ready for so much upheaval again. I need to build trust with everyone; I am sick of being weak and letting people down or letting them control me. I am my own woman now, and if you respect me, you will give me the space to understand my options and make an informed decision based on many factors, not just lust and the love of a fantasy."

Elizabeth jumped up, covering her nakedness, ashamed of her actions of the night before. Patrick looked startled and

THE PRICE OF SIMPLICITY

disbelieving at what he had just heard. Patrick had expected some resistance, but once they began to make love, Patrick had felt sure that Elizabeth was his and his alone. Elizabeth's doubts riled Patrick, and he thought about Richard in that house with those children he neglected. He would make sure that Richard never had Elizabeth again, he would make sure Richard left her alone, or Richard would die regretting it.

Patrick looked up at Elizabeth, standing and shivering whilst covering her body with the blanket she had swept off Patrick, leaving him exposed and beginning to react to Elizabeth's nakedness. Elizabeth was aware of the movement and looked down, eyes opening in distress, which jolted her to act, reminding her of her vulnerability. "Please, Patrick, don't make this any more awkward."

Patrick stood, ignoring Elizabeth's blushes; a new man had been awakened in Patrick; he felt this new man was more assertive, wiser and more steadfast. He was no longer insecure about his body in front of a woman; Patrick considered Elizabeth his, so she must accept all of him without qualms. Elizabeth would need time to adjust, and Patrick would always be loving and courteous to Elizabeth and the children. Still, Patrick would run out of patience if she kept him waiting too long. , After all, this was his calling, he had been re-born, and if he was to be the master of his own destiny, then she would have to be his mistress.

ABOUT THE AUTHOR

Shelagh Taylor

Shelagh, an accomplished writer, profoundly understands the myriad of unexpected challenges that life presents us with. Drawing from personal experiences and a keen sense of introspection, she weaves narratives that resonate with readers on a deeply human level.

With an acute awareness of the complexities of navigating life's trials, Shelagh skilfully explores the intricate interplay between reflection and the necessity of making on-the-spot decisions. Her insightful storytelling delves into the depths of human emotions, illuminating the choices we make and the lessons we learn along the way.

With each work, Shelagh imparts a sense of authenticity and relatability, captivating readers with her ability to bring the complexities of human experience to life.

Shelagh is a single mother of four adult children. She began university to study for a BA(Hons) in 'Youth & Community Work' when her youngest child was in high school. Shelagh then began working with at-risk children and families professionally. Shelagh immigrated to New Zealand, and after working with victims of domestic violence, she returned to university, where she completed a 'Primary School Teaching Diploma' as part of her mid-life reinvention.

With each book I write, Idiscover more about myself and strive to develop my strengths whilst addressing my weaknesses.

THE SIMPLICITY CHRONICLES

'The Simplicity Chronicles' is a captivating exploration that delves deep into the intricacies of life, unravelling its complexities and revealing the profound challenges that shape families.

Set in 1960s Yorkshire, this series delves into a family's fight to overcome the loss of their child, forbidden love and the entanglement of life.

The novels pose thought-provoking questions about choices and consequences, delivering a heart-wrenching narrative balancing humour and heartbreak in the Ryan family's struggles.

Obstacles threaten the family's progress as themes of resilience, betrayal, and sacrifices in a complex world are explored.

As the resilient women of the Ryan family confront uncertainty, love, and the consequences of their choices, "The Simplicity Chronicles" takes readers on a gripping journey of redemption, resilience, and the enduring power of survival.

My Sister Maggie

In the first novel, "My Sister Maggie," we are introduced to the Ryan family, whose matriarchs dominate the younger generations lives with their strong personalities and determination to dictate their futures.

Elizabeth Ryan, one of the main characters, leads a sheltered life until she meets Danny Ryan, a handsome, Irish, Catholic immigrant. Together they navigate the hardships of starting a family and surviving on very little money. However, as the story unfolds, we begin to see Elizabeth's forbidden love and the guilt that torments her.

Set in 1960's Yorkshire, with connections to a small Northern Irish town, this is a family's fight to overcome the devastating loss of their child. The impact of the loss spreads throughout the family, resulting in marital disruption, depression and health problems that affect not only the parents but also the surviving children who must live with the guilt of moving on.

Simplicity And Complexity

'Simplicity and Complexity' is a captivating and emotional story of Maggie Ryan and her family. The novel takes us to Northern England in the late 1960s and follows their struggles with poverty and hardship. Themes of love and loss, courage and strength are explored in a beautiful, heart-breaking way that will keep you reading. Highly recommended, Simplicity and Complexity is a must-read.

The family was known for their protection, but a secret lurks within the shadows. The protagonist Patrick Herron, reveals that as a young man he was victimised and abused, locked in metaphorical chains and subjected to mental and physical abuse and rape. He was filled with hatred and despair, while those around him pretended nothing was wrong.

The secret eventually came to light, leading to a murder and a trial. The stigma and shame of the crime weighed heavy on the family, as the court heard of the innocence that was taken away.

The story explores the depths of male rape, abuse and hatred and shows how it can tear apart even the strongest families.

However, Elizabeth still finds herself unable to let go of her feelings for Patrick Herron, the priest who captured her heart many years ago. As she tries to move on, she is faced with unexpected obstacles that threaten to derail her progress.

Printed in Great Britain
by Amazon